Nightshade

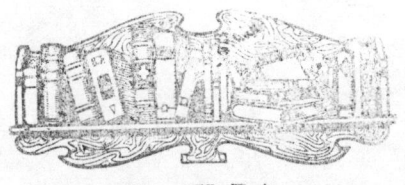

Roy W. Price

Also by Derek Marlowe
A Dandy in Aspic
Memoirs of a Venus Lackey
A Single Summer with Lord B.
Echoes of Celandine
Do You Remember England?
Somebody's Sister

Nightshade
by Derek Marlowe

The Viking Press/New York

Copyright © 1976 by Derek Marlowe
All rights reserved
Published in 1976 by The Viking Press
625 Madison Avenue, New York, N.Y. 10022

LIBRARY OF CONGRESS CATALOGING IN PUBLICATION DATA
Marlowe, Derek.
 Nightshade
 I. Title.
PZ4.M3488Ni3 [PR6063.A655] 823'.9'14 76-2396
ISBN 0-670-51418-7

Printed in U.S.A.
Second printing before publication

Acknowledgment is made to Penguin Books Ltd. for a quotation from "Poem" by Hugh Sykes Davies, from *Poetry of the Thirties* edited by Robin Skelton (1964), Copyright © Hugh Sykes Davies, 1936. Reprinted by permission of Penguin Books Ltd., and the author.

To Foscombe

HE: I sometimes wonder whether all those things you said were true.
SHE: What difference does it make? We both believed them.

Contents

Part One: Dainty Hungers   1

Part Two: The *Houngan*   47

Part Three: Enemies   83

Part Four: Late Sister Blanche   111

Part Five: The Ninth Day   153

For the Curious   191

Part One: Dainty Hungers

In the stump of the old tree, where the heart has rotted out,/ there is a hole the length of a man's arm, and a dank pool at the/bottom of it where the rain gathers, and the old leaves turn into/lacy skeletons. But do not put your hand down to see, because

1 It was going to be the happiest of times. The boat, the tumblers empty now of rum but each containing a single flower the colour of lenten purple, passengers sitting side by side not looking at each other but at least in a parallel direction, the sudden appearance of the twin volcanoes they had all come to see. They were smaller than they had imagined, but that didn't seem to matter any more. They were simply an excuse for the journey, two peaks rising out of the sea, one beside the other, encouraging bar-room pleasantries and laughter and shy smiles.

"They're called *pitons,*" somebody said, and a woman laughed again as the captain appeared and told them that two days earlier a small plane had crashed into the volcanoes, killing the occupants. That the bodies were still there. Instinctively, the passengers looked up at the land, quieter now, then turned away self-consciously and concentrated on adjusting sandals, preparing sun-tan oil, or merely staring at the sea.

Edward watched all this from where he sat by the rail, then studied his wife as she posed in profile, eyes lowered, hand reaching out to calm the pages of a book fluttering at her feet. It was going to be the happiest of times.

You see, it had to be.

The tropical port of Revenants was the second largest on the island, a small inlet set beneath the volcanic peaks with a bay deep enough for fishing boats and motor launches and perhaps a medium-sized yacht. Centuries ago it had been a garrison town for the French, but little remained of that now, apart from the courthouse, a cannon or two, a prison used to pen imbeciles, and a small square in the centre of the town, where the islanders would meet on special occasions, would put on uniforms and wear medals and parade up and down for an hour when the sun was low.

When tourists arrived, they would disembark at the jetty in the morning, then nervously huddle together into a pack as they hurried past the tin shacks, past the chipped enamel signs advertising Bovril and Typhoo Tea (beads from the British), and past the black faces that stared at them from verandas, steps, and the shadows of doorways. They would say to themselves that they wouldn't stay long, would hold camera and handbag tighter, and some would regret coming at all. But then, of course, they would convince themselves that this was Civilization, not some uncharted tract of jungle, that this is what they had paid for, what they had all looked forward to. And yet England, somehow, seemed so *very* far away.

Whether these feelings affected the latest arrivals, it was naturally difficult to tell. The glasses of planter's punch had helped to some extent, as well as the sun and the jokes and the quiet feeling of superiority. Most of the men, in cotton hats and shorts, were now standing on the jetty throwing coins into the water to be caught by small boys, both modest and naked, who scrambled over each other, dived and reappeared, some with coins in the hands, some in the mouth.

Edward didn't notice tham at first because he was gazing at the town. It was not attractive in the Romantic sense, but then it never claimed to be—being merely a fishing port until the tourists arrived. Whether it resented that fact is unclear, but certainly houses had been painted in ochre and russet, and a restaurant had been opened on a second floor, where gingham and flowers were on the table and an amateur landscape hung on a wall. It reminded Edward of Lake Como, absurd as that may seem. He had once visited there to explore the gardens in Bellagio and Cadenabbia and wasn't disappointed—a statue by Canova had been discovered in the coolness of an atrium, white within white. There were no gardens at Revenants, not in the European sense; but there was the water and the jetty and the hills beyond, and in that there was a similarity. *Greedy. Full of dainty hungers.*

"It's rather like Lake Como," Edward said, turning to his wife.

"Is it?"

"In a way."

He was about to elaborate, to describe the roses, oleanders, the hotel where Madame Solario took tea, when he saw the shoal of boys. They were in an arc below him, arms raised, and were chanting, "Small change, Charlie? Small change, Charlie?"

Edward stared at them, confused, then glanced around him, but he suddenly seemed to be alone. He saw smaller boys climb onto the shoulders of others, saw their black oilskin bodies, heard the chants, and he started to reply, shake his head; then as the arc grew closer, he retreated across the deck only to find other hands reaching over the rail and tugging at his shoes. He began to panic, stamping on the fingers as if they were ants but the hands were everywhere, scratching at his legs, at the turn-ups of his trousers, and pulling him towards the water. *Oh God, I can't swim. Why are they doing this to me?* A boy, naked and no more than six or seven, had now clambered onto the deck itself and was walking towards Edward, grinning at him, hand outstretched.

"Small change, Charlie? Small change?"

"Go away," Edward shouted. "Don't you know I can't swim?"

"Small change, Charlie?"

He looked around for his wife (Amy) but she had gone below to collect a cardigan and a hat.

"Go away," he repeated, throwing his arms out helplessly, then turned to escape as other boys, more confident now, viewing and perhaps enjoying Edward's embarrassment, appeared on deck and surrounded him. He turned once again (it all seemed so absurd—they were just *children*) when suddenly a voice said quietly:

"Just give them a coin."

A man was now standing a yard away dressed in a light cotton suit and white silk shirt.

"Wha'? Wadje say?"

"Just give them some money," the man said, smiling. "That's all they want."

Then, as if to demonstrate, he threw a handful of coins into the water and immediately the deck was emptied as the boys dived back into the sea and were gone.

"That's all."

The man smiled again, studied Edward for a moment, then turned and walked away just as Amy reappeared.

"I have your camera," she said. "Here it is."

They had been married four years but they were not, like many other people, surprised when each anniversary appeared on the twenty-first of December. They simply opened the cards, read them out loud to each other, then placed them on the piano, one within the other, between table-lamp and vase. Then, after a week, Amy folded them all together again (there were never more than five or six), levelled them on the polished wood, and placed them neatly in the righthand drawer beneath her sewing-machine, because she couldn't bear to throw them away. Each year she did this, and each year she was surprised to find that the previous cards from younger anniversaries were no longer there. But she never said anything because it didn't seem to matter at the time.

They had met at Hampton Court just before the Easter holidays, two people walking in their separate entities, guidebook in hand, gazing at beds and tapestries, one absorbing the fanfare of history, the other wanting to reach out and caress the damask between finger and thumb. It is doubtful whether they noticed each other immediately, for neither of them was demonstrative in appearance, being simply a face in the crowd and preferring it that way.

Naturally one could attribute this to shyness, but it was more than that. Edward Lytton, for that was his full name, was one of those men who considered ostentation vulgar, not only outwardly but inwardly. It embarrassed him, often noticeably (blushing came too easily to him—even to see the word in print caused him visible discomfort), and so he avoided it, guiding his life by what he considered *discipline*. Discipline of the mind (the Catholic Church had held the stirrup for that one), discipline of the body, and discipline in choice. It is an unfashionable philosophy but it suited Edward, and none of us ought to be so prim as to condemn him for that. After all, the poor man knew no other.

As for Amy (*née* Asbury), we must be careful not to truckle to our sentimentality, to mist the lens. It would be too easy to cast her as a heroine of that clergyman's daughter, present her with a Darcy or a Hampshire squire and be done with it. But that would be unkind as well as anachronistic: for Amy has charm, hidden at all but the most relaxed moments, but it is there. Charm and intelligence and not a little beauty—though not the Roxy beauty of the cotton-and-denim Boudicca or the muslin looks of her titled half-sister. Amy's are softer, unselfconscious, if she is conscious of them at all; a short nose, eyes that ought only to be appreciated in gouache or be seen in the shade of a pergola, a wide mouth, upper lip shading lower, jaw a little too round. As a child, Amy could have been drawn by Millais, if he was so inclined—the name Amy is deceptively apt—but though the plumpness remains, not much but some, the ringlets have gone to be replaced by curls the colour of cinnamon.

It must also be added that she is, by nature, passionate, though one could be forgiven for not realizing it as one observes her now. It is a private and sensuous passion that neither she nor anyone could explain. Her body fascinates her, the nakedness of it, while its sensations disturb her. They always have and they always will. Her hands have explored her skin, have baby-oiled it, abused it, observed it, wide-eyed, teeth over lip, a heart-stopping gasp as she hears footsteps on the stairs, her mother calling her once again to dinner. She has woken at night to find her night-dress on the floor, her body moist, and once when she was younger she had undressed in a neighbour's field, removing everything, including her watch, and lay, amid cow-parsley and dead bluebells, listening to a tractor navigating a nearby hill. Unremarkable perhaps in this Sweet Age of License, but to Amy it was the apogee of pleasure, clandestine as it was; and for that reason she never repeated the incident on that spring day, for she believed she could never be as happy again, reliving it only in her dreams, both day and night. Her only regret was that she lost the watch (a present from a favourite cousin), and to this day it has not been found.

But whatever the outlet of Amy's desire, however suppressed and introvert (unlike her late sister, Blanche), it was there within her. And that in itself is enviable. Odd then that she should choose to stop, turn her head, and talk to Edward, who had never exhibited even a sigh of passion in all his three and a half decades of existence. Odder still that she should marry him before the year was out. But that was the way it was.

For the record, Amy at Hampton Court was nineteen years old, daughter of a Gloucestershire landowner. She was also a virgin.

As, of course, was Edward.

The port of Revenants was now below and to the right of them. The passengers were all sitting in a truck, opposite each other, knees touching, as they were being driven up the narrow road between banana trees, now and again passing one of the islanders holding a machete or swerving to avoid a stray dog.

"The island is full of dogs," somebody said.

After half an hour they stopped on the edge of a plateau, and everyone got out, husbands helping wives, and stood in a group. It was the smell they noticed first, a gasping acrid odour that distorted their faces. Someone likened it to brimstone.

"Sulphur," the guide said, gesturing towards the yellow crystalline rock on each side of the road. He then walked to the beginning of a path, stopped, and said, "You must all follow me. You must keep to the path or you will be burnt. The water in those pools is very hot. More than boiling point. Very hot."

"Then it *is* like brimstone."

"Yes. Perhaps."

The passengers immediately stared at the rocks and pits and the water bubbling within them, blanketing the sky with steam. It was explained that it was the volcano that created the heat, and a story was told of criminals long ago (murderers, felons), being taken up to this spot at night and never being seen again. It was probably an apocryphal story, told with great delight by the guide, but the tourists accepted it because it was what they wanted to hear. It added an ingredient of danger, something to write home about.

"Do you think it's true?" Amy said, gazing at a nearby rock-pool, then looking back at her husband when there was no answer. He wasn't looking at the sulphur or the water but at the passengers, then back towards the truck.

"What's the matter, Edward?"

"There seems to be somebody missing."

"Who?"

"Another man. He was on the boat. I talked to him. I thought he was sitting in the front. With the driver."

"What man?"

"How many were there on the boat?"

"Eight. No ten. Counting us."

Edward glanced at her, then counted the other people who were now walking in a single file behind the guide, walking down into the plateau itself. There were eight of them. Four husbands, four wives.

"It doesn't matter," Edward said. "He probably lives in the town."

It was arranged that they would eat in the local restaurant before returning to the boat. They had visited the sulphur springs, and then the mineral baths, where Edward took a snapshot of Amy standing before a waterfall; then another one, just in case the first one didn't come out. The mood was now lighter, voices louder, and people used first names and discovered those small coincidences of mutual acquaintances in Dorset and Stow-on-the-Wold. Edward and Amy, naturally, stayed together, walking side by side, and when someone asked Ed-

9 Dainty Hungers

ward what he did, he simply said *Antiques* and left it at that.

At the restaurant, they sat opposite each other near the shutters above the street, not saying a word, but keeping their hands politely on their laps as plates were laid and menus placed in front of them. Small wooden boards the shape of a tarpon.

"Your face is getting brown," Amy said finally.

Edward looked at her and she smiled quickly and concentrated on the menu, a shallow frown appearing between her eyes. That finely etched *W*.

"What's *accra chou*?" she asked, without raising her head.

Edward didn't answer but simply observed her, the shutters patterning her face into parallels of light and dark. His gaze descended slowly down her hair onto her neck then on to the pale blue cotton shirt she had bought the day before at the shop near the hotel. It was unbuttoned, not indecently, but just to the breasts. Three buttons, no more, revealing a triangle of skin lighter than Cotswold stone. Edward stared at it for a long time, at this discreet portion of his wife's body, divorcing it from the whole, a detail in a canvas reproduced to reveal the brushstrokes, the texture, the blending of pigment within pigment. It was as if he was seeing it for the first time, but it was not the pores and gradients that he observed, not the *physical* sense at all. It was the touch. The sensation of touch, even though his fingers rested on nothing, brushed nothing, not even each other. He felt her skin. That's what it was and he couldn't describe it any other way. Sitting in this ridiculous restaurant in the middle of the Tropics his hand was touching his wife's skin. Her body. Just there.

"*Accra chou* are cakes," he said. "Small crisp cakes made from *tanias*."

The years that followed their wedding were singular only in their conformity. Day passed day after the honeymoon (they had spent the occasion in the Loire Valley visiting the châteaux, one after the other) and to describe one is to describe the sum. Edward had his job at a London Auction House of Some Repute which he fulfilled diligently and with passing recognition. His speciality had been Victorian Art, but then, as time passed and fashion outgrew his taste, he retreated into the nursery of Illustrated Books for Children (plus Juvenilia), white quartos of Dulac and Rackham in their original ties. It was a bizarre choice when one considers Edward's life, for there were never any children to see the books or touch them, nor did it seem as if there ever would be.

On a few occasions, Edward would bring a volume home, just for the evening, carrying it in his briefcase, then opening it after he had washed his hands, placing the book of pictures and text on the table. He would turn back each tissue and each page, his index finger hovering over a bewitched tree, a Rhine Maiden, a Moloch, reading an italic out loud and looking up at his wife and repeating the phrase. That, you see, was how blind the man was. He never realized what he was doing, not even for a moment, and Amy knew it. That is why she forgave him. *It was other women who had children.*

At first, however, she thought circumstances might change, for that is often the nature of things. Perhaps it was the rural background that produced the optimism (the purchase of lawn-sprinklers during a flood), for certainly the honeymoon had not been a success. In a sense, it was understandable, for God knows neither of them had a precedent as far as the nights were concerned. But there was more to it than that. They never touched. Edward never touched, never made the advance, and it is possible he never even wanted to try. He was Ruskin (a critic), if you wish, with a knowledge of the female body confined to naiads and water-sprites, bald from the neck down and coddled in gossamer. It seems impossible to contemplate it for we are talking about today. But it had to be so.

Of course, one can offer Freudian interpretations, medical diagnoses, but, whatever one says, the fact is that Edward saw Amy naked only for a moment—she had undressed slowly in front of him aping something she had read in a magazine bought at Kemble Station—and he had turned away, banishing her from his vision, shocked at this overt side to her nature. He couldn't cope, didn't know how to, while

Amy had only the experience of dreams. It was tragic. There is no other word for it, and, inevitably, it could only get worse, until even the everyday bodily functions of his wife horrified him. It need not be said, therefore, that after this pitiful overture, both slept separately, first in different beds, then in different rooms, Amy moving into the spare room, the one she had decorated in pink.

And then, as if in recompense, they both became the best of friends.

That really is the heart of the matter. They *were* friends, enjoying each other's company more than anyone else's, sharing the platonic experiences of garden and museum (Sissinghurst was a favourite of the former, Greenwich of the latter), visiting and revisiting without loss of enthusiasm. People who knew them envied them, cited them as a "happy marriage," and if strangers thought them to be father and daughter as they stood side by side considering the Cube Room at Wilton, neither appeared to take offence.

"She's my wife," Edward would say, a slight blush. "Amy's my wife."

And she was. Though not in the eyes of the Church, which insists on Consummation (that coy word) to sanctify the vows. Edward knew that too well, but fear had become habit and the door remained closed. He didn't know what was happening in the adjacent room. How could he? He wasn't capable of visualizing the fantasies that inhabited Amy's mind as she lay in bed, her night-dress still neatly folded under her pillow.

Fantasies of liquid the colour of magenta, a pomegranate redness, viscous to the touch, so that one has to lick it dry, finger and thumb, falling like rain, a vertical cascade, falling into a plain that resembles a battlefield. Fantasies of drums, chants, screams, shapes glimpsed in a mist like night creatures scraping the soil as they scurry away, peeping above things and under things, shoulders, the bridge of a nose soaked in scarlet. Of spears and halberds and pikes, a picket fence railing the horizon. Fifes, whistles, a pitch that only hounds can hear, and yet *she* can; decibels, splintering in her mind. Fantasies in which she cannot move, can only stare at the sky, at the liquid, cannot close her eyes.

Where her arms, hands, legs, hair are thumbtacked, nailed to the earth, hammered into the ground like Gulliver on that island, impaled around her, and she feels them, *feels* them, creatures, spiders, incubi, snakes, feels them moving into her body, searching, prodding, under her clothes, into the heat, *heart,* heat, caves, hair, sliding, burrowing within her, her stomach swelling, stretching *(An heir! My God, what AM I?),* stretching until she knows it will split like a sack of grain, spilling out grubs, winged insects, gyres and gimbles, rip open as the heat increases, and she hears the screams, shouts, a tractor on a hill. Fantasies that choke her, smother her, and burn her.

And fantasies that end in the quiet sound of water seeping into pebbles. And the distant pulse-pulse of a cicada.

Now how could Edward, the poor wretch, expect to understand matters such as these?

"I think we ought to go if we are all ready."

The captain of the boat was standing at the door of the restaurant, in the frame itself, so that the plastic streamers (red, green, yellow) that hung as a form of ventilation were draped over his head and shoulders. At the base of each streamer were small bells, no larger than a thimble, tinkering one against the other.

Everyone stood up, replaced chair under table, thanked the restaurateur, whispered about a tip, then walked down the narrow stairs into the bleached light of the street. It was now three o'clock in the afternoon.

Edward and Amy were the last to leave, a quiet contentment. It had been an unusual meal, foreign naturally, but not too forbidding. Each course had been explained in the nicest possible way, and if a pawpaw or a breadfruit had been left on the side of the plate, no fuss was made. Edward had appreciated that, and had written down the name of the restaurant on a blank page of his pocket diary.

Outside, the air seemed cooler—though the shadows on the dust of the road were finely focused, unbiased negatives of the people, both white and black.

13 Dainty Hungers

"Did you enjoy the meal?" Edward asked.

"Very much," Amy replied. "You?"

"Very much. It's a pity we will never come here again."

"Won't we?"

"Probably not."

Edward smiled sadly and looked away, and they began to walk slowly towards the jetty, keeping to the centre of the road, not looking to the left or right, but concentrating their attention on the backs of the people in front, as if everything outside this chosen corridor was alien territory. It was then, just as they reached the edge of the row of houses, as they stepped from shade into sunlight, that a voice called out to them. At first, Edward ignored it, assuming it to belong to a beggar or a drunk. But the voice was repeated, more insistent, and then he noticed that Amy had stopped and was staring towards the corner of the building.

"It's just a beggar," Edward said, walking faster.

"No."

The word was said quietly and without hesitation. *No*. There was no defiance in the tone. Just a simple statement of fact. It was this attitude, on what appeared to be a trivial incident, that startled Edward to the extent that he himself stopped and turned, looking not in the direction of the voice but at his wife.

She stood quite still for a moment, then slowly did the most surprising thing, at least it was to Edward, for there seemed no cause for it. Without saying a word, she raised both her hands and took the large straw hat from her head and held it by her side, so that her face and hair were suddenly exposed, almost as though she were revealing her features for the first time. A mundane action, as these things go, the removal of a hat; and yet Edward suddenly felt afraid.

Later, when he was alone, he recalled that moment and realized that it was the same emotion that he had experienced on his wedding night. But Amy wasn't naked, not even remotely so. In fact, she was more dressed than that wretched woman from Esher who had sat next to him on the boat. The removal of a straw hat. What a petty overture for a farce. No more, it is said, than the breaking of an eggshell.

Edward was now staring towards the building twenty yards away. He couldn't make out the owner of the voice at first—partly because of what he felt, and partly because the light was in his eyes. Then, finally, he saw him, the man who had appeared on the deck and had thrown the coins to the boys. He was leaning against one of the iron pillars of a veranda surrounded by the dark shapes of some islanders, leaning casually, arms folded. In appearance (the pose, the features—though the skin was somewhat darker than European), the man reminded one of the subject of a miniature by Hilliard, vain and yet mesmeric, to be observed behind glass. This image might have occurred to Edward as well on a more impartial occasion, though Tudor Art had never been to his taste. He, perhaps, would have seen the man drawn by d'Orsay. And quartered too, no doubt.

"I asked if you were enjoying your holiday."

The voice was soft, a slight accent that was probably French and not unpleasant.

Edward felt his face reddening, hated himself for that, and replied quickly, "Yes. Yes, we are."

He wanted to leave but he found he couldn't move; the very act of moving an inch seemed to be under scrutiny, like a tightrope-walker who has suddenly stopped in the centre of the spotlight without the faintest idea of what to do next.

"Will you be here long? On the island?"

"No . . . Not long."

"And then you will go home?"

"No."

"You will go somewhere else?"

"Yes."

"Another island?"

"Yes. Another island."

"Perhaps we will see each other again."

The man was now running the tip of a petal over his arm as if tracing out an imaginary tattoo.

"We must go. The boat . . ."

Edward gestured vaguely towards the sea. He was conscious of sweat on his back and under his arms, settling onto his skin like polar insects. He turned in the direction of his wife, wanted to take her hand but hurried away, back towards the boat that seemed to be a mile away. At one point, he thought he'd never reach it and that he would walk forever. That the jetty, sea, boat were just a mirage. It was as absurd as that.

Husband and wife didn't talk until they were at sea; the town of Revenants was hidden by a promontory, and only the twin volcanoes remained as a backdrop. The other passengers were also subdued, but theirs was a quiet dictated by the sun, a soothing after the meal and the tour.

Edward and Amy sat apart from them at the stern of the boat staring at the wake and an occasional glimpse of flying fish that had ceased to attract curiosity. Nobody bothered to count them any more.

"I suppose he must live in the town," Edward said finally.

Amy didn't answer.

"Did you notice something?" he asked. His wife was sitting, legs outstretched, parallel, her skirt tucked under her knees. On a toe of her left foot was a strip of Band-Aid. The fourth button of her shirt was now undone. Probably by accident.

"That man," he continued, "he put his arm around the other man's waist. Did you notice that, Amy?"

Later, before they arrived at the hotel, Edward asked the other passengers about the man but none of them had seen him. They said they were walking ahead and never noticed.

All this took place on a Thursday.

2

On Friday, Edward went for a walk alone. It was not of his choosing, this solitary promenade, but out of respect for Amy's health. She was not feeling well. She mentioned the sun and everyone agreed that the heat could be tiresome if one was not used to it. That and the food.

"I'll just sit on the patio and read a book," she said.

A novel by Maurice Baring was taken from a drawer. Petit-point prose of embassy daughters with pale hands, now quietly out of fashion.

"I'll be all right. I'll just sit here and read."

It seemed for the best, and Edward reluctantly agreed. You see, he never could bear being apart from his wife, not in the waking hours. He needed her beside him, a companion to share the small experiences of the day, no matter how trivial. In a sense, she was the only friend he had, and without her he simply felt alone. Lonely. Solitude would depress him, even for an hour; and if she went out he would stand at the window of the house, watching the road until she returned, appearing first beneath the racemes of a laburnum. Admirable, perhaps, this canine devotion, and yet he never once revealed this side of his character to Amy. He hid it—hid it as if it were a secret fetish to be kept behind lace curtains, too proud to declare this basic need to the only person who was close to him. When the fool did, of course, it was too late.

"Keep in the shade," Edward said, adjusting a canopy. "Promise me that."

The hotel was laid out in a semicircle so that all the guests could see the ocean if they so wished. Within the embrace of its walls was a palm-lined terrace, a small hibiscus garden popular with hummingbirds, an open-air restaurant, and a swimming pool used in the main by small children and Americans. Beyond that, to the west, was the beach and then the sea, close enough to be heard at night if windows were left open.

Edward walked to the corner of the hotel, past couplets of canvas chairs, past the shouts and the laughter, and then turned back and looked towards the patio. He could see Amy sitting under the tasselled umbrella (cornflower blue to match cushions and tablecloth), the book open before her. She was wearing a white dress with an olive-green pattern (scrolls and petals), her hair loose, and as she sat there, her left hand unconsciously reaching up to touch her neck, she looked very young. Almost a child. On an impulse, Edward wanted to return to her, sit next to her, and ask her again how she was. But he didn't. He simply took a photograph of her instead, replaced the Kodak in its case, then walked away onto the gravel path that led on to the cliffs above the bay.

It was almost three hours before he returned. The path had been deceptive, unravelling slower than it had appeared, so that by the time Edward realized the extent of the journey, it seemed pointless to turn back. And so he continued to the summit of the cliffs, a steep face inhabited by gulls, and stood for a moment at the top, breathless, his feet among burnt grass, and considered the view, a requisite chore.

It was not spectacular in the classic manner; it was merely the sea seen at an elevation, and in that it was disappointing. Nevertheless, Edward snapped it as a keepsake for the winter, then decided to return to the hotel. From where he stood, the path meandering below him, it seemed as though there was a shorter route (the roof and one of the cabanas could be seen to the right), not by descending the cliff but, instead, walking along its edge, then through a wood which appeared to emerge above the beach. At worst, the distance would be the same and there would be no fear of falling.

Within half an hour he was lost. There was no doubt about that. *I should have stayed with Amy,* Edward said out loud.

He was now in a field amid some kind of crop that was possibly maize. The sun had reached its height, eliminating shadows, burning into his skull and shoulders through his poplin shirt. *It was all so foolish.* He thought about retracing his steps, but he had read somewhere that that was often a mistake, and that he should stop and "take stock." The hotel was on the west of the island, but then so was he. Then it still must be to the west of him (wasn't there something about using a watch as a compass?), west of him and below him. Edward looked around, the green needles of corn above his waist stretching out in each direction, barely disturbed by the wind, a mere *frisson* touching the surface and nothing more. He listened for the sea but that was no longer audible (he couldn't have walked *that* far), having been upstaged by the sound of birds and insects. Beyond a ridge a car could be heard for a moment, gears cancelling gears, and then it was gone, the drone fading, and there was silence.

Curiously, Edward felt no concern about the situation, but rather inquisitiveness tempered with irritation. He recalled a line of verse his mother had written on Basildon Bond (she had been a minor poetess, who had once aspired to be in the same paddock as the Bloomsburies but mercifully failed), a stanza about a scarecrow. It was symbolic, naturally, but that was how Edward felt, standing in the centre of a field in the middle of an island. Like a scarecrow. A Worzel Gummidge. Strange, these unexpected childhood echoes at a time such as this.

Edward dismissed the thought and was about to continue (the car indicated a road; he would plump for that) when he heard a moan. It was unmistakable, as if an animal had been caught in a trap. A low moan, close to him. Edward paused and slowly looked around until he saw, at the edge of the field, that the corn was moving, not naturally but as if something hidden was shaking it. Not a small animal like a rabbit or even a dog, but larger. Immediately he wondered what creatures could inhabit such an island; he had never really thought about it before, except to be warned about snakes and tarantulas. But whatever was there, within reach of him, was nothing like that. He should leave it alone, go away, and find the road. Indeed, Edward did walk away but then the moan was repeated anxiously, as if something was in pain. Calling to him for help.

Quietly, treading carefully on the ground, Edward turned, the sun and Amy forgotten, and moved back, drawn to the disturbance as though it were a cynosure. The corn parted around him, a bird suddenly screamed on his right and rose out of the earth into the air, a plant tugged at his sleeve, hesitated, then released it. He could smell his own sweat, hear his own breathing until ten yards away he could see the hollow and the broken stalks ahead of him. Five yards away he could see the creature within the hollow, and it was then that he stopped. There were two of them, black, one within the other, the man on his back, the woman between his legs in genuflection, head, neck, and mouth, the movement of a metronome.

Edward watched quite calmly (a cirrus of butterflies hovered above a naked back), observed what he couldn't understand, had never seen, not even in a lithograph. Never knew existed. *Dainty hungers.* Then he realized what was happening and the next moment he was not there any more. It was as though he had never existed.

"She went to the beach."
"What?"
"I think she went to the beach."

Edward blinked at the empty patio, then looked at a woman who was sitting by the pool wearing large oval sunglasses, reminiscent in effect of Little Orphan Annie. Both legs were in the water to just below the knees. Nearby, a child with a white hat on his head was walking out of his depth.

"The beach?" Edward said. He picked up Amy's book, straightened out a folded corner, then placed it neatly back on the table. In the darkened room behind him he had seen the white dress with its olive-green pattern lying on the bed. At first he had thought it had been Amy herself, and had asked it how it was feeling.

"That's the direction she took."

He had looked in the bathroom mirror to see if his appearance had altered, but it hadn't. There was just dust from the road and a scratch on his hand where he had run into brambles. The driver of the white Packard had said he owned a plantation that used to belong many years ago to Monk Lewis. The writer of ghosts.

"Is she your wife?" the woman by the pool asked, pushing up her sunglasses and squinting towards the patio. Two half-domes of blue paint could now be seen above her eyes.

"Yes."

Edward found Amy by the steps to the gardens on the perimeter of the beach. She was lying on a canvas seat, arms by her side, wearing a white one-piece bathing costume, the modest kind so popular during the War. Beside her was an identical canvas seat placed parallel to its partner but empty save for a towel draped over its back. It was Edward's shadow that touched Amy first (the sun now the stray's ally) causing her to raise her hand to her forehead, palm up, and turn her head.

"The woman said you'd be on the beach."

"Which woman?"

"I don't know her name. The one who plays the piano."

"I've been here all afternoon. I wanted to sun-bathe."

"But you can't swim, Amy."

"I didn't swim. I sun-bathed."

"Are you sure you ought to?"

A football decorated in black hexagonals bounced across the sand and landed in a shallow by Edward's feet. He stared at it, oblivious of shouts, calls from behind him.

"I thought you'd be back earlier," Amy said.

"I got lost."

Dainty Hungers

Edward glanced at her, then shuffled his gaze towards the sea. For a while he seemed to be in a trance unaware of the football being collected or of Amy standing up, pushing a cedilla of hair from her eyes. Then suddenly he turned and said, "I hate this island."

Amy looked at him, puzzled.

"But you liked it before. You said—"

"I hate it. It frightens me, Amy."

There was a long pause. Husband and wife stood without moving or saying a word, almost as if they were strangers. Along the beach a man was removing red flags from a box and laying them at intervals of twenty feet, ready to be planted.

"Only two more days and then we leave," Amy said finally, her voice quiet, reassuring. She didn't know what disturbed Edward, but she understood.

"I'm sorry," he said. "I didn't mean to spoil your day."

"Don't be silly. You didn't."

"I'll leave you to sun-bathe."

"No, I've finished. Two hours is far too long anyway. It was just that—"

"I know," Edward said and smiled, watching Amy as she collected her handbag and a plastic bottle of sun-cream. He studied her mouth, slightly parted, tip of tongue resting on the underside of the upper lip as she considered the colour of her right arm.

"It shouldn't burn," she said and then looked up and caught Edward's gaze, saw him blush, then looked away, and began to walk back towards the hotel.

After a moment, Edward called out to her, "Is this yours?"

He was holding up the towel from the neighbouring seat.

"No," Amy said, shaking her head. "It was there before I arrived."

Edward returned it to its place, folding it neatly, and as he did so he looked at the canvas on the chair. It was wet. Not all over but just in two patches, a rectangle and a divided oval, eighteen inches apart, one above the other, complemented by indentations as if someone had been lying there. Slowly, Edward lowered his hand and touched the lower patch, felt the dampness that was still cold despite the sun.

"Did you say you were on the beach all afternoon?"
"I can't hear you," Amy called out. "I'm in the shower."

Apple. Olive. Leaf. Grass. The pentimento of a wood, the branches of an ash merging through those of an oak. Curious that this verdure should be the colour of such a destructive emotion.
Green.
The colour of Eden.

On the last day on the island, the hotel gave a party for its guests. It was a traditional affair where the manager and the assistant manager wore white dinner jackets, and a Steel Band was hired from the capital. Tables were set out on the beach, a bonfire was lit, and there was a choice of chicken or steak. Rum was free.
In their rooms, Edward and Amy were sitting, each on their respective beds. The music could be heard (a naughty calypso) and a woman was laughing on the neighbouring patio.
"We don't have to go," Amy said. "We could stay here."
"It's not that."
"What is it then?"
Edward stared at a suitcase slumped over an armchair, ribbons touching the floor. He could see Amy's clothes arranged neatly on one side; her underclothes. He had once seen them in a drawer of her dressing table in England—he had been looking for a nail-file and had lingered—and had been surprised to see how fragile they were. A pair of pants, the triangle of nylon no larger than the flap of an envelope but black and bordered in scarlet. It was a startling revelation for Edward, this vulgar taste of Amy's for such an intimate garment. He couldn't understand it. As he looked at the suitcase he tried to rediscover the article but it wasn't there. Just uniform white. *Perhaps,* he thought, *she is wearing it.*
"Edward, we ought to at least eat. You didn't have any lunch."
Her books too. She never read the Baring, at least not all of it, preferring more contemporary romances, usually American. He had once found a popular paperback by D.H.Lawrence on the bathroom floor

and after that had decided to introduce Amy to Chesterton, a grammar school idol. But she had been a reluctant pupil, and when he had asked her to put down on paper what she thought of the writer, she had written: *G.K.Chesterton is fat because he did not reach the age of puberty until he was 19. He is a Catholic and known to be anti-semetic.* Now where, apart from the misspelling, did Amy learn things like that?

"We could go for a while," Edward said. "After all, it is our last day here."

"I'll have to change."

Edward looked at her, then said, "I'll meet you on the beach."

They really *were* the best of friends. It was madness for Edward to think otherwise. He told himself that a dozen times, attributing this unnatural suspicion to the heat, the island, and oh, a million things. Evaporation can be very deceptive. Besides, it had been their first holiday outside Europe since they had met, and it was obvious that it would affect each of their characters differently. Someone had told him, or he had read somewhere, that it was something to do with the light and being on an island. That it was like being on a boat during a long voyage. Commonplace behaviour suddenly appeared sinister. Whether it was true or not, Edward didn't care because he had decided to accept the theory. As Amy had said to him three months earlier, what had happened in Tewkesbury need never happen again.

The beach was now crowded as the party had graduated from polite banter to laughter and sidelong glances. In time the sea would attract the more daring and more drunken, and caves to the south of the bay would propose opportunities for future guilt. Edward himself drank little, sitting at one of the tables under the palms listening abstractedly to the conversations around him. It was meaningless gossip, holiday platitudes, though there was talk that the bodies from the crashed plane had still not been recovered from the volcano. A man and a woman.

While waiting for Amy, Edward found that he was obliged to endure the company of two people from England, a Mr. and Mrs. Parkins. He (Parkins) had a book-jacket face, pleasant enough but looking as though he never perspired. This was not a profound observation but only what Edward cared to notice. Parkins merely passed away the time.

"You're leaving tomorrow?"

"Yes," Edward said, peering through the half-light towards the hotel. He could see silhouettes and shadows.

"For England?"

"No. We're doing a tour."

"Oh. And why are you doing a tour?"

"Because we—well, prefer not to stay in one place."

"And *where* are you doing a tour?"

"The islands."

"Which islands?"

"Well, they're not *all* islands. Not really."

Parkins stared at Edward, assessing him, then lit a panatela (baby eyes unblinking), holding the cigar in absurdly white hands. A woman of repute had once said that out of all men she couldn't imagine Parkins naked.

"Are you married?"

"Yes."

"Is that your wife over there?"

"Where? No."

"And where is your wife?"

"In the hotel. She'll be here soon."

"And what is her name?"

"Amy."

"And is she English?"

"Yes. Yes, she is."

Edward might also have been interested to know that Parkins, as well as being tiresome, at least to men (wives, it is rumoured, would lunch with him daily, one place or another) also claimed to be a Catholic Marxist. It is a fashionable equation so little more need be said about that.

"And why did you come here?"

"I told you. Just a holiday."

"To see what we once had?"

"We?" Edward asked.

"The British. The island was British once. Didn't you know that?"

"I thought it was French."

"The filthy French first, then the British. Now it's anybody's."

Edward nodded, disinterested, and glanced at Parkins' wife. She was sitting patiently, a docile addendum to her husband and nothing more. As Parkins' monologue grew, was embroidered and became more dogmatic, she would play her minor part (Babs to the magician), presenting an accompanying smile to the audience. And if the questions became more personal (as they invariably did), the smile would change imperceptibly, would widen like that of a dowager whose poodle has just soiled the cushion. Baby didn't mean it.

Edward studied her, not listening to Parkins (politics was now centre stage, Religion in the Wings), but letting his mind wander. Perhaps it was hearing the news of the plane crash that made him suddenly recall a story about a funeral: A Widow weeping by her husband's grave was approached by a Gigolo who whispered words of love through her veil. Naturally, the Widow turned on him angrily, chastising the Stranger for being so heartless on such a Sad Occasion. *I apologize, madame,* the Gigolo said, *but the power of your beauty overcame my discretion.* To which the Widow replied, *You should see me when I have not been crying:*

It was a pleasant enough story, and Edward tried to remember where he had read it or who had written it, when he became aware that Parkins was no longer talking. Instead, both husband and wife were looking in his direction, not *at* him exactly but past him.

"Is something the matter?" Edward asked.

Parkins' wife said there wasn't but that they had just seen a woman whom they had observed the day before and had remembered her because she had been such a fine swimmer. That was all.

"Oh, I see," Edward said, relieved, and turned casually, arm on chair, to find himself face to face with Amy.

She was standing before the bonfire so that patterns of crimson and vermilion were flickering on her face and hair. Behind her was a constellation of sparks against the dark sky. Edward made no immediate attempt to attract her attention but turned back to the table.

"Excuse me . . ." he began.

Parkins and his wife however were no longer there, for they were now sitting alone at another table beneath a lantern hanging from a tree. From their attitude it seemed as though they had been there for some time.

"I didn't keep you waiting long, did I?" Amy asked as Edward approached her.

"No, of course not. I was talking to two people from the hotel. They live near Burnstow."

"I've never been there."

"No. Nor have I."

Edward stared at her, then said, "Well, shall we eat? Join the queue?"

They each took a plate and held it in their hands as they lined up to be served. They talked of small matters, the weather and the music. Somebody was already in the sea, fully dressed.

Then Edward said, "You didn't go swimming yesterday, did you? While I was away."

"Swimming?" Amy replied, laughing. "But you know I can't swim, Edward."

"Then it must have been somebody else."

Later, they sat side by side, watching the other guests as if they were performing on a stage. It was Amy's analogy (She liked games. Bear that in mind.) and she enlarged it by attributing roles to the people around them as if they were all stock characters in a parish play—Duchess, Bishop, Butler, Murderer, and so forth. At one point Edward saw Parkins talking at a pretty blonde girl with porcelain features and grateful eyes.

"What about him? Who would you say he is?"

Amy glanced at Parkins.

"Oh, Village Policeman," she said dismissively.

"And the girl?"

"The Victim."

27 Dainty Hungers

"Too obvious."

"Too obvious?"

"Don't you think?"

"Oh. All right. The Murderer then."

The game was played with variations but nothing that could be considered intellectual, since Amy, as has been observed, was never that. That, it is sure, would have spoiled her; hardened her perhaps. It is difficult to say. Certainly, Edward would never have married her if she had been as intelligent as Edward thought he was himself. He couldn't have tolerated this equality, for discussions would have become arguments, and, in time, they would no longer be friends but rivals. Amy was just sufficiently perceptive and attentive to give Edward the feeling of confidence he needed; and if at times she wasn't as eager an apprentice as he might desire (the Chesterton incident, for example; or the Beethoven episode that obviously needs no further discussion), then Edward accepted it with grace, a tolerant mentor. The games, *her* games, were what is commonly described as "parlour." Harmless nonsense that required Imagination rather than Honours.

"That woman over there. Pink dress."

"The Vicar's Wife," Amy said. "Tipples on sherry."

"Good touch. What about the woman with her?"

"Left or right?"

"Left. Not *her* left—"

"Our left. Downstairs Maid. No, they usually have no chin. Some kind of maid though. Perhaps Housekeeper."

"Lives in?"

"Oh no. North Lodge. Cleans the candelabra, gossips in the village, and steals the spoons."

Amy giggled and poured another glass of wine. Edward smiled and looked around, seeking to select a more difficult character, someone more elusive. Then he saw him, stepping out of the darkness, his face first in profile, then turning towards him. At first he wasn't quite sure where he had seen the man before and his immediate thought was that it had been in Europe. Somehow he associated him with an abbey, for bizarre reason. But not an English abbey. More Byzantine in design, an image of stone, louvered windows, and painted pillars. Then the man smiled, and he recognized him and blushed instinctively at the memory of the port and *Small change, Charlie*? He was the person from Revenants.

"What about *him*?" Edward said, pointing towards the man standing no more than twenty feet away. "What would you say he was?"

"Who?"

"The man there. In the beige suit and white shirt."

"Whereabouts?"

"There. I can't point too obviously because he's looking at us."

Amy followed Edward's gaze, staring across the sand.

"Beige suit?"

"Well, brown then. He's looking straight at us."

Amy frowned.

"No idea?" Edward asked.

"I can't see him. You mean near the bonfire?"

"No. Just in front of us. You must be able to see him."

"You mean the man wearing glasses talking to—"

"No!" Edward said, irritated. The man now looked amused and was chewing idly on a leg of chicken he had taken from the barbecue. "Look in the direction *I'm* looking. See?"

Amy shook her head. "Is he white or black?"

Edward sighed and said, "You're doing this deliberately."

"I'm not. Honestly."

"It doesn't matter. He's walking away now."

Edward stared at his wife, then she suddenly turned and grinned.

"Amy," Edward said, smiling back at her. You and your games."

It was quiet now. The music had stopped and the band had gone, leaving only a circle of embers in the sand, a gentle hiss as the tide eased over it, retreated, and returned. The beach was deserted except for one or two lovers, a minimal movement, merging into shadows, fingers against skin, the perennial etcetera. A dog, two dogs, a man with a bald head standing in the surf discovering the moon. The sound of insects. A woman's voice being heard, for a brief moment, raised in accusation, from a hotel room, a slamming of a window, and then silence.

Edward lay awake in the room listening to Amy breathing, asleep in the next bed. He had tried to sleep himself and for a while had succeeded, but then awoke as if out of a nightmare, expecting to encounter figures, shapes standing by his bed and leaning over him. Children in a field glimpsed from a carriage, beckoning to him. He had wondered where he was, surprised to see his wife (they had, of course, not shared a room for years) and had felt afraid. At one point he had got up, treading on Amy's shoe, and had stared down at the adjacent bed. He had watched her move in her sleep, turn over, legs and body outlined under the sheet, and he had suddenly leant over and moved a wisp of hair from her eyes. But she didn't react.

Returning to his own bed, Edward lay awake until the sun rose and he could hear the hotel waking up, the sound of water-sprinklers pattering on the terraces and amid shrubbery. Today they would leave the island, would take the plane and fly north; but he had no regrets. It had been an uneasy week; and he knew that if they had stayed longer, a day even, something sinister might happen. He couldn't explain why, for there was no logic in his fear; it was just that he felt nervous.

Careful not to disturb Amy, Edward now put on a towelling robe over his pyjamas and walked out onto the patio, closing the door behind him. The light was already bright and reassuring, and he found that he was the only person awake, up and about, except for two of the hotel staff, one attending to the pool and another sweeping under the restaurant tables. Edward said, "Good Morning," pleasantly, and began to stroll across the tiles on the terrace, stopping to admire a flower or observe a humming-bird, the contours of a leaf lanceolate. After a while, feeling more relaxed, he walked, hands in pockets, onto the beach itself, the sensation of sand under his bare feet, and stood gazing at the sea. Somebody else, it seemed, had also had a sleepless night and could be seen swimming out towards a marker-buoy.

Edward stood and watched him, admiring the man's skill, until the swimmer returned, heading for shore, allowing the action of the tide to carry him onto the beach. He lay for a moment in the surf, then stood up, pushing hair away from his face, and walked to where he had left a towel, picked it up, and saw Edward.

"Couldn't sleep either?" the swimmer asked.

"No."

The swimmer nodded as if he understood, took a watch from the towel and placed it back on his left wrist. With the towel was a book: *Gevoy Nashego Vremeni*. He then walked up the beach, and as he passed Edward he stopped and said, "We keep meeting each other. Don't you think we ought to introduce ourselves?"

"Edward Lytton."

"Daniel Azevedo."

The two men shook hands politely and Edward said, "Do you live in Revenants?"

"Not any more."

Edward studied him, noticing the pale blue eyes, surprising for his skin colouring, and a small scar above the left eyebrow. The nose of Brummell. Then Azevedo smiled and walked away, stopped, turning into profile, and said, "Perhaps we'll see each other again soon."

"I doubt it. You see, we're leaving today."

But Azevedo appeared not to hear and was already moving into a mist on the higher land and onto the grass leading away from the hotel towards the cliffs. Edward watched him till he was no longer in sight, then returned to the hotel and his room.

Amy was still asleep, lying on her stomach, one hand touching the floor. It was now six-fifteen in the morning. A Sunday.

At ten o'clock Edward was standing at the hotel desk signing Traveller's Cheques to pay the bill.

"Don't you think we ought to leave a forwarding address?" Amy said. "Just in case."

In the taxi to the airport, Edward was silent, staring out of the window at the huts, women with bundles on their heads, abandoned cars lying by the roadside covered in weeds and flowers, both inside and out, like surrealistic sculptures. For some reason, Edward never mentioned the meeting on the beach. It seemed superfluous and yet he thought about it.

And then as they passed a church he said, "I'll miss Mass today. The first time in ages."

There was no reaction from Amy and Edward glanced at her. She was sitting very still, staring ahead of her and appeared to be very pale despite the suntan.

"What's the matter?" he asked anxiously.

"I've forgotten my hat. The straw hat."

Edward laughed. It seemed such an absurd thing to be concerned about, and he said so. But Amy didn't relax, behaving as if it was the most important thing in the world. The misplacement of a hat. Before them on the dashboard of the car the driver had stuck a pattern of coins, a rash of cents and pennies and francs covering the area between speedometer and glove compartment. Before the windscreen, a plastic *Vierge*.

"We can't go back to the hotel now," Edward said. "We'll miss the plane."

"I don't think I left it in the hotel. I think I left it at Revenants."

"I'll buy you another."

The island was beneath them now and they could see the bays and the twin peaks rising to the left, almost vertical, then dropping back quickly, wiped away, as the LIAT jet, pink in colour, banked, rose, and settled into its flight pattern.

It'll be all right now, Edward thought.

But of course it couldn't be. Not now.

"There it is," Edward said.

"What?"

"Haiti."

Not any more.

3 The man was waiting at the airport desk as he always did; skin blacker than most, a small man in a white double-breasted suit and carrying a cane (part of a collection) between thumb and middle finger, holding the ebony stick with only the slightest pressure of his fingers, as if it were a rare and rather precious vial. He was a vain man, familiar to tourists and more especially their wives and daughters, welcoming their arrival to Haiti like a Georgian blackamoor opening the door and unfolding the steps of a caleche. His name was Lapôtre, and when the Lyttons arrived at Duvalier Airport he kissed Amy's hand.

"Where are you staying?" he asked in French and then repeated it in English.

"At the Castelhaiti," Edward said. Around him faces stared at him, muscular young men in shirtsleeves leaning on the customs barrier. On the wall a photograph of an old man with spectacles and grey hair.

"Castelhaiti?" Lapôtre said, looking at Amy. "No, you must stay at the Grand Hotel Dessalines. It is *my* hotel. *The* hotel. It is where you must stay."

"But we are already booked at—"

A snapping of the head, a petulant sulk, then Lapôtre said, "I will arrange it personally. You will stay at the Grand Hotel Dessalines."

"Thank you," Amy said, smiling, and glanced at Edward.

In the taxi to Port-au-Prince, Edward took off his jacket and tie and lowered the windows because of the heat.

"Do you think he was . . .?" Amy began.

"What?"

"You know? What you said. A Tonton—"

Edward glared at her and pointed a finger cautiously at the driver.

"What?" Amy asked, frowning.

Edward pulled another face, clenching his teeth and widening his eyes in a grotesque caricature of caution, then saw the driver staring at him through dark glasses in the rear-view mirror.

"Oh, don't be silly, Edward," Amy laughed, fanning herself with the pink Carte d'Identité.

From the beginning it had always been Amy's idea to visit Haiti, despite Edward's reluctance. He had told her the usual stories and read out the usual accounts of torture and suppression and secret police in open-neck shirts; but he had seen by her face that it made not the slightest difference. It excited her, though not the danger itself, for she never accepted that there was any. It was more the chance of doing something that one ought not to do (at least in Edward's eyes), something forbidden, like catching trout out of season. In a sense, it was an act of defiance on Amy's part, wife against husband, and why Edward finally agreed to add Haiti to their itinerary is a mystery. Perhaps he simply wanted to prove to Amy that he had been right, hoping that she would want to leave after the first day (he had taken precautions for that event), and would therefore never oppose him again.

And yet, on reflection, that sounds too severe. It makes Edward out as a dictator, some kind of bully, and he was never that. In all probability, having decided to undertake the extravagance of this holiday, Edward merely wanted to do everything to make Amy happy. He had promised himself that after that wretched evening after Tewkesbury, when she had burst into tears, gasping for breath. Frightening him, so that he could only stand at the door and stare at her helplessly and watch the pain. "We'll go away, Amy," he had said the next day, telephoning during his tea-break. "We'll go away to the sun."

The journey from the airport to the Dessalines took forty minutes, driving south through the town of Port-au-Prince itself, the mountains on the left and the sea on the right. Edward and Amy talked little, except to comment on the heat, and once Edward remarked that he hadn't seen any beggars, unlike on the other islands.

"They're too poor to beg," Amy said.

"What does that mean?"

"They're too poor to beg."

"How can they be too poor to beg?"

"You can be too poor, *so* poor that you can't do anything. Anything at all."

"But not too poor to beg. To beg is to be poor."

"Poverty often demands action. But extreme poverty negates all action. Even begging."

Edward stared at his wife as she looked at him, chin up, a slight trembling.

"Amy," he said, smiling. "Now who in heaven told you that?"

"Extreme poverty" (a slight stammer), "extreme poverty negates all action."

"Oh, that's nonsense, Amy."

Amy studied him for a long time, then finally faltered and lowered her eyes.

"I must have got it wrong," she said quickly and turned back towards the window as they passed the Cathedral, a white domestic fabric reminiscent, if seen from a distance, of its namesake in Paris.

The taxi, a Peugeot, now entered the main avenue of the capital, past statues of revolutionaries rather badly carved, railings, the Presidential Palace itself (precocious toy) and then, within minutes, the road became narrower, tarmac was replaced by gravel and, in turn, by loose stones, and houses were no longer brick but wood, banked in tiers on the side of the mountains. They paused to watch a funeral procession, a solemn extravagance of plumes and brass amid the rubble and the dogs. Old men removed their hats and a woman was glimpsed in the back of a limousine. She wore a white headdress, as if she was going to a wedding. Edward asked in French who had died, and the driver pointed to the coffin and drove on.

More houses, more dogs, chickens and pigs, a billboard informing the people that Jean-Claude Duvalier is their idol, and a rare piece of graffito on a wall written by a brave punster initialing the capital city into a statement of truth: *P-au-Pèrisme.* Then finally the taxi was bumping over potholes and turning into a driveway amid palms and stopping before a baroque edifice, a picture-book fantasy of balconies and towers and wooden cloisters.

"Is this the hotel? *Est-ce l'hôtel?*" Edward asked.

"*Oui. C'est l'hôtel*"

"It's the hotel, Amy. Who would have guessed?"

But Amy was already standing at the foot of the steps, staring up at the bleached pillars and wooden lace hemming the terraces. She appeared mesmerized, looking not as if she was seeing the building for the first time but more as if she had envisaged it many times in the past, perhaps in her imagination, and was not disappointed.

"It's sure to be expensive," Edward said. "Maybe we should stay at the other hotel after all."

Amy smiled and slowly caressed the carving on the balustrade with the tips of her fingers.

"That man at the airport, Lapôtre . . ." she said quietly.

"Oh. Him."

"He was right. This *is* where we should be. He knew."

Edward stared at the hotel, unsure.

"I still think I ought to ask how much it costs. I mean, look at it."

He hesitated then began to walk away when Amy put her hand on his arm.

"I'll be happy here, Edward. You'll see."

Edward stopped. In the hotel someone was playing a piano. A song by Gershwin.

"Will you be, Amy?"

The driver had now taken the suitcases from the taxi and was standing, watching them. A redheaded girl appeared from the direction of the swimming pool, stopped as if suddenly remembering something, then turned and hurried away.

"Yes."

They were informed at the desk that they were expected (a telephone call from Lapôtre) and that they were to stay in the Valentino Suite, named after the actor.

"He once stayed here," the desk clerk told them in a slow, Linguaphone voice. "Many years ago he stayed here with his second wife. She was called Natacha Rambova. When you see the rooms you will see a photograph of them both. They are in profile. When Valentino died, the hotel was draped in black and no one swam in the pool for eight days."

Amy seemed enchanted by the story and thanked the desk clerk twice, while Edward signed the register, relieved to see a comforting pedigree of English names (Ashburnham, Dowson, Anthony Last), and wrote in fine copperplate the two names separately, one above the other. They were then taken, following their suitcases, past the potted plants, the piano, a portrait of Phoebe Stanley, two Americans dithering over backgammon, and along the wooden cloisters that comprised the hexagonal of the hotel.

"I don't understand why they are treating us like this," Edward had whispered, pretending to admire a fuchsia. "They must have confused us with someone else."

The suite of rooms was at the eastern corner, somewhat isolated and yet with a view over the town and the bay. Ships could be seen and a stadium and beyond that the Cathedral they had passed earlier.

"Of course that wasn't her real name."

"Who?"

"Her real name was Winnie Hudnut."

"Who?"

"Natacha Rambova."

A photograph was referred to on one wall beneath a print by Philome Obin. Amy glanced at Edward and smiled, then sat down on a large brass bed, decorated in sylvan motifs and hung with a mosquito net. In an adjoining room, much to Edward's relief, there was its partner.

"Valentino slept in *your* bed, madam."

Amy made no indication that she had heard, but watched Edward as he took his suitcase through the partition and placed it emphatically on a chair. In the past, of course, the Lyttons had both been obliged to share the same bed as the Guests of Friends in The Country, but the occasions had been few, and Edward had taken note. He had felt self-conscious lying in the same bed as his wife, aware how unnatural that was, and so had not complained. Instead, he had deliberately retired late, replacing the board-games into the cupboard and turning off the lights, and had risen early, rarely sleeping in the hours between. He had not commented on this to Amy, nor had she made any sign that she was aware of the rarity of the situation, obvious as it was; she had simply been asleep when Edward went to bed and asleep when he awoke.

Nevertheless, Edward hated these nights because he felt guilty, difficult as that may be for you and I to understand, exceptional beings that we are, devoid of inhibitions as we pose like the Missionary or Dear Little Fido and lollop between the sheets. But that is the tragedy of it all. He felt this guilt as he lay still, staring at shadows on the ceiling or into unfamiliar corners of the room; he would hear Amy's breathing, feel her turn over, sigh in her sleep, sense the warmth of her; and sometimes she would unconsciously touch him, a limb, an unidentifiable angle of her body straying against his, cotton pressing against cotton, and Edward would tense, not move, like a field-mouse sensing the presence of a hawk. Then in the morning, dressed and in daylight, the guilt would be gone. He was once again on equal terms with the world. At one point in their marriage, Edward had introduced Amy to a friend from school who had become a priest. Subsequently, Amy had asked her husband if *he* had ever wanted to be ordained. Edward had said no—adding that he had felt unworthy for such a vocation. That he was too weak. This conversation took place ten months before the incident in Tewkesbury.

"Please enjoy your holiday in Haiti."

"Thank you," Edward said, tipping the porter a dollar.

The door was closed, leaving them both alone. Nothing was said for a long time, nor did either of them move, as if posing for a daguerreotype. Two people, identity unknown, occupants of a room in Hispaniola; a composition distinguished by the smile of the woman, a quiet mischief visible only to the viewer.

The next morning, Edward believed he saw a man on the balcony just outside their room.

It was a Holy Day, spelt out in red on the Catholic Calendar, and Edward eased his soul by attending High Mass at the Cathedral. Amy didn't accompany him nor did he ask her; he had tried years ago to lead her on the Path to Rome, had lent her his red pocket catechism *(Edward E. Lytton, Form IVB)*, but she had asked too many questions he couldn't answer without raising his voice, and then seemed to be only interested in Torquemada and the Burning of Witches and such like matters. "There are things I will never know about you, Amy," Edward had said, taking the books back and leaving her only with a rosary as a keepsake.

From the hotel be took a taxi to the Cathedral, surprised to see how Catholic the country was, passing women in white, with white headscarves, and clutching prayer-books and followed by children in their best suits and starched dresses, small girls in white Topsy ribbons. At the Cathedral itself, other cars drew up, many of them military, a horde of uniforms in bottle-green and blue. It was said that the President For Life would attend, but Edward didn't see him, even though he waited on the steps beside the pink pillars until he heard the Mass begin.

When he left it was midday, and he had to walk to the main square before he could find another taxi to take him back to the Dessalines. He had prayed for Amy as he always did, as well as for his mother and his father, Amy's late sister, Blanche, and for himself. It was then, as he was stepping out of the taxi, stepping onto the driveway of the hotel, that he saw the man. He had turned to hand the dollars and

39 **Dainty Hungers**

gourdes to the driver and had raised his head over the roof of the car. It was a subconscious action, as when one senses someone is watching just outside one's eyeline, and he had looked up quickly to catch sight of the balcony and the figure of a man leaning over it, as if keeping surveillance.

Now Edward at this precise moment was unusually relaxed (the celebration of his Faith always had a soothing effect), and consequently his reaction startled him. He knew that he was not yet familiar with the layout of the hotel and that all the balconies looked the same. Nevertheless, he experienced a sudden feeling of panic, and stood back to try and put the mosaic of windows and terraces into perspective, allowing his mind to retrace the interior of the building, the corridors he had walked, until his gaze returned, as he feared it might, to his own room and the balcony itself. By then, of course, it was empty. As were all the others. He had made a mistake. It was another suite. He had imagined it all.

"Is my wife still in her room?" Edward asked. He was now standing at the desk, leaning on an angle to it so that he could see the lobby and the lounge beyond. A middle-aged Creole in a Disney shirt was playing the piano as he had done the evening before. Prohibition jazz.

"My wife? Mrs. Lytton?"

The clerk glanced at the board behind him.

"Well, the key is here."

"*I* put it there."

"Then I couldn't say, monsieur. Do you want me to call your wife?"

"No, it doesn't matter."

In her room, Amy was sitting at a table writing a picture postcard to her parents. She was wearing a crimson bathrobe she had chosen herself. The postcard was a colour glossy of *Le Nègre Marron*. A statue.

"You're not dressed," Edward said.

"I'm sorry. I was writing letters."

"You could have dressed, Amy."

Edward looked at her, then walked across the room towards the balcony. The dividing door was closed, cutting out the sun. He was about to open it when he stopped:

"I can smell cigarette smoke."

Amy looked up and frowned, nose tilted like a Bisto Kid, stared intently at the ceiling for a moment, then finally shook her head. No.

"Well, *you* don't smoke," Edward said. "And *I* don't smoke."

"Mmmmm?"

"I said *I* don't smoke."

"Are you sure it's cigarettes? It could be the room. Or outside. Bonfire."

"No. Bonfires are different."

"Then perhaps it was the maid. She could have been smoking."

Edward glanced at Amy's bed, neatly made up, night-dress folded over pillow.

"Well, even if she did, you would have seen her, Amy."

"I was in the bathroom. Out of the way."

Amy smiled, catching Edward's eye.

"Open the shutters. The air will soon get rid of it."

On the balcony, Edward could see the driveway and the cars turning around an island of lawn and eucalyptus. He could also see the other balcony directly above him and stared up through the slats at the gridiron of blue sky.

"I have made a mistake," he said.

"What did you say?" Amy called out.

The powder resembled a terrapin, though the body or shell was narrower, more oval in design. The head and legs could be clearly seen, though the tail, assuming the creature *had* a tail, was eclipsed by the base of the sink. It was swimming/crawling from mirror to door, its right feet touching the wall of the bath, its stomach encircling the mat. The imprints in the centre have been made, of course, by human feet, two in number, both left and right. Toes can be distinguished if one kneels down, taking care not to disturb any of the talcum; though the impressions are not clearly defined, merely round indentations, like eyes on a domino. It is here then that she stood after emerging from the bath, the left leg apparently being lowered first. A ringlet of water and an italic *c* of hair that has stubbornly remained on the base of the tub to bother the aesthete. She had stood like this, and had seen her reflection in the mirror as she reached out for this towel. It is interesting how it is almost dry, unlike a canvas chair under the heat of the sun.

Edward waited on the main terrace of the hotel while Amy dressed for lunch. A few minutes earlier, Lapôtre had arrived accompanied by a tall Negro smoking a small clay pipe. He was not introduced, but later Edward learnt that he was a *houngan*, a voodoo priest.

Lapôtre himself had smiled, asked Edward how he liked the hotel, had inquired after *la belle Madame Lytton* ("She is not ill? She is so pale."), and had walked away, one hand on the shoulder of his companion. Edward watched as Lapôtre stopped before a woman who was crossing the lobby carrying a souvenir (a mahogany quaich); she stopped, and he took her hand and kissed it. The woman had blushed, unsure of how to react, then stood self-consciously as she was handed a flower from a buttonhole and Lapôtre stared up at her, leaning on his ebony cane. She was embarrassed but flattered, as Edward could see. Just as Amy had been.

"He was just being kind," Amy had said the previous evening. They had gone for a walk after dinner in the gardens of the hotel. A French couple had invited them to play bridge but Edward had declined.

"But you allowed him to kiss your hand, Amy."

Amy had laughed, that four-bar allegro that lately had begun to irritate, followed by the inevitable phrase: "Don't be silly, Edward."

"You mustn't be jealous," Amy had added after a moment. "He's far too ugly."

It had seemed to Edward that that was an extraordinary thing to say. It implied an alternative, a hypothesis. He had wanted to comment on the remark but the realized he was being foolish. Amy was Amy, and it was absurd to talk of jealousy or whatever. The word was superfluous between them. Didn't exist. What is more, he loved his wife more and more each day, and though he hadn't told her that fact, he had written it down in his diary and that was what mattered.

"We're very lucky, aren't we?" Edward had said as they had returned to the hotel to sleep in their respective rooms. Amy had smiled, and as they had entered the main lounge, where all the other guests could see them, she had reached out and taken his hand.

Someone else was now playing the piano (a painted upright), an American in a dark suit, unshaven, the face of a vain pugilist, cigarette in his mouth. He was playing something unrecognizable, possibly original, and behind him sat a fair-haired girl in a pleated skirt. Edward heard her praise the music and then the reply: "It stinks." The American then talked of the Fates, the Destinies, his voice soft and nasal, an accent from the Lower East Side of New York.

"They've been at me now nearly a quarter of a century," he said, not looking at the girl. Nearby, four or five people watched, as if in an audience. "First they said: 'Let him do without parents. He'll get along.' Then they decided: 'He doesn't need any education. That's for the sissies.' And right at the beginning they tossed a coin—heads he's poor; tails he's rich. So they tossed a coin—with two heads. Then, for the finale, they got together on talent. 'Sure,' they said. 'Let him have talent, but not enough to let him do anything on his own—anything good or great. Just enough to let him help other people. That's all he deserves.' When you put all this together, you got Michael Borden."

"Oh, Mickey," the girl said, applauding and encouraging the others. "You remembered every word."

After ten more minutes, Edward decided to call Amy on the housephone by the main desk. There was no reply for almost a minute, causing Edward to peer around the lobby—in case she had just appeared. Not seeing her, he was about to put down the telephone when it was answered.

"Yes?"

It was Amy's voice but it sounded startled and out of breath.

"Amy?"

"Yes?"

"Are you all right?"

There was a pause and a muffled sound as if a hand was being placed over the receiver.

"Amy? Are you still there?"

Another sound (telephone being dropped?), then:

"I'm sorry—what did you say?"

"Amy, are you all right?"

"Yes, of course. I'm almost ready."

"You sounded out of breath."

"I was in the bath."

"In the bath? But you've already had a bath."

"In the bath*room*."

"You said 'bath.'"

"Bathroom. I'm nearly ready. I'll be with you in a minute."

Edward hesitated, then said, "Well, hurry up, Amy. I've been waiting an hour."

But the phone had been put down. Edward stared at the receiver in his hand and then carefully put it back in its cradle.

"Thank you," Edward said to the desk-clerk, and was about to move away when he stopped and asked on impulse, "Could you tell me who's staying in the room above ours?"

"Which room is yours, monsieur?"

"The Valen-Valentino."

"And you want to know who is in the room above?"

"If's possible."

A glance at the keys and the register.

"That would be Mr. James, monsieur. But he checked out half an hour ago."

Edward stood on the gravel where the taxi had stopped and recreated in his mind the action of turning, visualizing the driver, raising his head. A slight misfocusing as his eyes rested on the leaves of a cedar, then on the balconies themselves. Coloured towels were hanging out to dry like carnival banners and someone was adjusting a folding chair. The sun, however, created too many shadows for Edward to see the building clearly, and so he decided to walk along one of the paths fronting the hotel. His behaviour was becoming farcical, and

Edward knew it. But he had to reassure himself, had to be content that he had made a mistake over such a trivial matter. *The Discipline of the Mind.*

The paths crossed and recrossed, narrow stone lanes descending into gazebos and follies, so that anyone walking along them for the first time would suddenly encounter a statue of a minor goddess, say, or a Caucasian nude, and then after a few minutes would confront the statue again, but from a different perspective, the spine rather than the face. One would have to stop, look around for the guidance of the hotel, then begin again. As Edward did. Though he was not lost as he had been on the other island, but simply confused.

At one point he heard voices and laughter, recognized it to be a swimming pool (bounce of feet against wood, silence, silence, splash), and found himself standing on violet tiles, feeling conspicuous in jacket and tie. Nearby the girl with red hair, observed on arrival, was standing in a dry bikini, left foot scratching right calf, holding a transistor radio to her ear. To her right, a middle-aged American in a Budweiser hat was reading *Sports Illustrated.* Counter-clockwise, three women, like the Three Graces, lying on back, stomach and back; a black barman, a drink trolley, a quartet of Germans playing poker very noisily, a man with an arm raised holding an empty glass, a Latin sneaking glances at his own body. Two more women. Edward. Girl with red hair. On the surface of the pool, a Lilo supporting a young man in denim briefs; underneath, the sole swimmer, the man who had dived and was now underwater, an Impressionist daub of buff and blue, swimming strongly from north to south. It was he that Edward was watching, a sudden feeling of gaping recognition, of *déjà vu.* The image of a beach appeared in his mind and a man swimming towards a marker-buoy in the early morning. He began to feel hot, almost suffocating, and repeated to himself that it couldn't be; that he was allowing his imagination to create illusions. *It couldn't be the same man.* And then the swimmer in the pool surfaced and it wasn't. It was a stranger, a man with a moustache whom Edward had never seen before in his life. He wasn't even remotely like the person who had been haunting Edward's wretched dreams. Not in any way. Besides, Daniel

Azevedo was nowhere near the pool. He was, in fact, standing by the steps of the hotel. That's where he was.

"Hello, Edward. I told you we would see each other again."

Surprisingly, Edward was unable to think of a single thing to say.

Part Two:
The *Houngan*

In the stumps of old trees, where the hearts have rotted out,/there are holes the length of a man's arm, and dank pools at the/bottom where the rain gathers and old leaves turn to lace, and the/beak of a dead bird gapes like a trap. But do not put your/hand down to see, because

4

"But it must be more than coincidence, Amy. I'm sure he must be following us."

They were sitting in a corner of the restaurant, husband and wife. They had chosen Jambalaya from the menu and then had changed their mind and settled for Creole Gumbo, a shellfish soup seasoned with okra and powdered sassafras.

"He must have found out where we were from the forwarding address," Edward continued." Do you remember, you told me to leave it?"

But Amy didn't appear to be listening. She was remaining in profile, gazing out across the lawns towards the town.

"He must have gone to the Castelhaiti and they told him we were here."

This latest encounter with Azevedo had in fact been as brief as the others. A greeting, a polite inquiry into Edward's health, and a casual invitation to accompany him on a tour of Kenscoff, a market town in the nearby hills. Naturally Edward had declined the offer immediately, saying that he had "things to do." It was a lie, of course, and it was apparent that Azevedo sensed it, but he made no comment, merely smiling, bowing, and walking away. If you are English, you will understand this caution on Edward's part; it's in our character and that really is all that need be said. Except that Edward secretly regretted the refusal. Worse, if he was honest with himself, he knew that he had wanted to see Azevedo again from that very first meeting at Revenants, though one hastens to warn the less prurient reader not to sigh and hurl the book out of the conservatory window. It was just that Edward disliked most people he met, because he felt, perhaps erroneously, that most people he met disliked *him*. Daniel Azevedo was simply an exception. Nothing more. Which is why Edward stammered his refusal to this offer of friendship. You see, he just couldn't cope with it.

"His name is Daniel Azevedo. At least that's what he *said* his name was."

A smile appeared on his wife's face, and she turned towards Edward with the expression of someone who is politely tolerating a pedantic anecdote by a child.

"He didn't seem surprised," Edward said, lowering his voice, glancing around. "Didn't seem surprised at all. It was as if it was the most natural thing in the world, suddenly turning up like that. That's what makes me sure that he's following us. Amy—"

There was a sudden sound of laughter and Edward stared at his wife, startled by her reaction.

"What are you laughing at?"

"You, Edward."

Edward blushed.

"I don't think it's funny. I don't—"

The waiter appeared at the table and set down the plates and a basket of garlic bread. Amy said thank you and the waiter nodded and moved away.

"I just don't think it's funny, that's all."

"He's just a tourist. Like us."

"But why the same places at the same time?"

"It's a free country," Amy shrugged.

"No, it's not—" Edward began then stopped and smiled. Wine was ordered. When it arrived, Amy said quietly, "Is he staying in the hotel?"

"I don't know. I don't think so. His name wasn't in the register."

Amy glanced up, eyebrows raised.

"Well I looked," Edward said. "Just to see."

"Oh, Edward, why should anyone be interested in people like us?"

"I don't know."

"It's just coincidence," said Amy.

Edward didn't eat, but merely sat and watched his wife, who suddenly seemed to have an appetite for two, dipping the ladle once more into the tureen, fingers seeking out a scroll of prawn or the delicacy of a crab. She appeared to be unconcerned, someone on holiday, accepting matters as they were, with the minimum of fuss and outward panic. Edward had noticed in his quiet way that there were certain women who always had that ability to adapt to unfamiliar surroundings, as if it were the most natural thing in the world; to blend in immediately to the background without any apparent effort—like a camouflaged animal or bird. Amy was like that, especially here in Haiti. It was as if she belonged.

"If only he wasn't so polite," Edward said, and glanced at his wife as she broke off a piece of bread to soak in the plate. At a nearby table, Lapôtre was posing for a Polaroid taken by the woman he had approached earlier, the flower from his button-hole now entwined in her hair like a gymkhana rosette. So weak, Edward thought. The woman was so weak, for could she not see how foolish she was?

"Baby octopus," Amy said, holding up the fork vertically to bisect her face. "Try some."

Dainty hungers.

"No thank you."

Amy narrowed her eyes and smiled, a glisten of soup on her chin, then carefully placed the cylinder of black flesh between her lips, resting it on her tongue for a moment before allowing her mouth to close. Later, coffee and cheese.

Azevedo now appeared to be forgotten, at least on the surface, though he was seen a second time during the meal. Edward had been gazing over Amy's left shoulder, daydreaming.

His mind wandering.

Images of England.

In the foreground of the first is an empty croquet lawn, mallets lying on the grass together with someone's abandoned sweater; behind it, hollyhocks, both pink and white, and then the figures themselves sketched in lightly, unfinished, so that the pencil-marks are still visible. Two people, a man and a woman, are sitting on cane chairs drinking Pimm's served from a jug, Sunday papers lying by their feet. A routine cliché, perhaps; but it is deceptive, for you can now see that a second woman, almost identical to the first and probably a sister, is removed from the others and is now watching them from a bedroom window—or, more accurately, she is watching the man. The face is finely detailed, brushstrokes emphasizing the eyes and mouth, as if the artist is anxious to record the expression before it fades. It is the focal point of the study that is tentatively entitled "The Week-end after Tewkesbury."

Another image, then a postcard. This one:

My dear Amy,

Do you recognize this? I tried to find one of Hampton Court itself but they only had this photograph of the Chapel. Wilkie thinks we ought to get married there! How are things in Glos? Give my best to everyone and tell Blanche we insist she is a bridesmaid

See you on Friday. Will take the
16:48 train
love,
Edward
P.S. Miss you v.v. much.

In a further image, the face at the window has gone and the curtains are drawn, even though it is only midday. Below, the garden is empty and a chair is overturned.

It was while Edward was thinking of Blanche that he had heard someone laugh, had realized where he was, and had seen Azevedo standing on the gravel driveway behind Amy. He was talking to two guests from the hotel whom Edward recognized as the American (Borden) who had been playing the piano and the fair-haired girl in the pleated skirt. Edward watched for a moment and saw the girl take off her hat and hold it in her hand. Azevedo then pointed towards the hills, smiled, and walked away out of sight. "He's found somebody else," Edward said to himself.

Amy herself didn't notice this incident, nor did Edward mention it. Instead, he dismissed it with reluctance and turned his attention back towards the table. After a while, they began to small-talk about the holiday, and Edward described the stained-glass windows in the Cathedral (Amy listening, chin on knuckles), and then he mentioned that he had met the *houngan*.

"Did you? Did you really?" Amy said with unexpected enthusiasm.

"You know what a *houngan* is?" Edward asked in surprise.

"Yes, of course I do."

"What is it?"

"What?"

"A *houngan*? You don't know, do you?"

"But I do."

"What then?"

"It's a kind of voodoo priest. The opposite to a *mambo*, which is a priestess. That's what it is. Isn't it?"

A reluctant "Yes," and then: "How did you know that?"

"Oh, Edward, I know lots of things. Why should you be surprised all the time?"

"It's just that . . . Well, I'm just surprised that's all."

Silence. A woman suddenly rushed into the restaurant, called out *"Petit Pol!"* twice, very loudly, then looked around and hurried out. Her footsteps could be heard on the steps.

"How did you know about these things?" Edward asked. "Voodoo and nonsense like that?"

"From Blanche. She told me."

Edward looked up, startled.

"Blanche?"

53   The *Houngan*

Walking into the curtained bedroom with a glass of Pimm's, groping for the light, Edward finds something banging against his face. Reaching up to brush it away he finds he is holding Blanche's feet, the left one now minus a shoe. *Oh dear,* he thought, *she's hanged herself.*

"*Blanche* told you?"

"Yes. She visited Haiti about six years ago."

"I never knew that."

"It was before I met you."

"But you never told me that. About her coming here."

"Does it matter?"

"Yes. No. I just didn't know."

"I thought she might have mentioned it herself."

"No. Why should she?"

"I don't know. Let's not talk about it."

"But you brought it up, Amy."

"I know I did but—"

"It was agreed that we would never talk about—"

"Please, Edward. Not now."

Amy closed her eyes for a moment, a slight trembling, then opened them and smiled.

"I'm sorry. I didn't mean . . ."

Edward nodded, glanced around him, then stared at the wall. Lapôtre, dear heart, had sent across two glasses of Grand Marnier as a special treat, and Edward and Amy drank them slowly, then ordered another in want of conversation.

Finally, Edward said, "Amy?"

"Yes?"

"No regrets?"

"About what?"

"About us. You and I."

Amy began to smile, then changed her mind, mouth descending to neutral.

"I shouldn't have asked that," Edward said quickly. "We promised never to analyse. Just to accept each other as—"

"Do *you*?" Amy interrupted, remaining in profile.
"About the holiday? No. Never."
"I thought you were talking about marriage."
"Oh." A silence. "No."
"No you weren't talking about marriage?"

"No. No regrets."
When they left the restaurant it was almost three o'clock in the afternoon, and they discovered that they were the only ones still there, waiters standing by the door.
"I suppose everyone must be having a siesta," Amy said.
In the lobby, Edward collected the key, while Amy went on ahead to her room. As it happened he was delayed (confusion at the desk), so that he was alone when he walked along the corridor and heard his name being called. At first he didn't hear it (he was thinking about trivial matters), and then it was repeated, a low whisper, a tongue pouting the consonants:
"Edward."
There was no one in the corridor, neither before him nor behind him.
"Edward."
A window was open, overlooking the hill behind the hotel, but as Edward looked out of it he could see nothing but a group of black children, a hundred yards away, playing an improvised game of football.
"Edward."
"Yes?" Edward said, spinning around, dropping the key, lunging for it, missing then grabbing it from the floor. "Who is it?"
The mesmeric chatter of insects, birds. A car door being slammed on the other side of the building. Standing still, listening, Edward looked around him. There was no mistake, and he knew it. He had heard a voice.
"Is there anyone there?" he called out, and then added, "Amy?"
There was no answer. *I must have made a mistake,* he said to himself in reassurance.

A door opened, and a woman appeared and looked at him as she checked her handbag. Edward recognized her as the girl with red hair he had seen by the pool.

"Hello," she said.

"Hello."

"Do you know if there's a Lloyds bank in Haiti?"

"No, I'm sorry."

"I have to send for some money."

"Why not ask at the desk?"

"I did. Do you speak French?"

"A little. School French."

"Me too."

A smile. Then: "Are you lost?"

"No."

"You're lucky. I've been coming here for years and I still get lost. Ever since I was a child."

Edward smiled and glanced along the corridor.

"You *look* lost," the girl said.

Edward stared at her.

"You looked lost when you were by the swimming pool."

She was tall, pretty in a fashion-plate way, and wearing a T-shirt upon which were written the words "August the Fourth" from one breast to the other. Levi's, sandals.

"No, I'm not lost," Edward replied. "I just thought I heard somebody calling me, but there's no one here."

"Oh, I hear voices all the time," the girl said. "Especially at night. Does it worry you?"

"A little."

"What did the voice say?"

"Edward."

"Is that your name?"

"Yes."

"My name is Alice. Hello again."

"Hello. Are you staying in Haiti for long?"

"Good-bye," the girl said and walked away.

When Edward arrived at the Valentino, he found Amy already sitting in her room, on the bed.

"Had my own key," she said, holding up the key in the palm of her hand, fingers parallel to the floor.

"You weren't calling me, were you?" Edward asked.

"No. When?"

"Just now."

"No."

They decided against a siesta, each in their separate rooms. They decided because they had been in the country for two days and really they had seen almost nothing, apart from the hotel and the view from the taxi. As Edward remarked, it wouldn't be a holiday if they hadn't even witnessed the views on the postcards. He held them up, then laid them on the table. This and this and this, he said emphatically. Or this—a photograph of the market at Kenscoff.

Amy, on her part, was apathetic about trudging from one edifice to another in the heat of the day. She would be quite content sitting still, on the balcony perhaps, taking in the sun and reading a book. A collection of paperbacks had been bought for this very purpose, a select mixture of thrillers, romances, and Books of the Film. At present she was halfway through *The Comedians,* because it seemed appropriate, but was unable to finish it because it was missing from the bedside table. "The maid took it," she said.

Edward himself read little fiction, preferring glossy tomes on Victorian Art or Definitive Biographies of errant Englishmen (Lawrence, Wingate, Burton, that kind of thing) or now and again something by those Catholics of the Lounge Bar—Chesterton, Belloc, Read the Younger, and the upstart waiter, Waugh.

"I do think we ought to go *somewhere,* Amy," Edward said. "We may never come here again."

"It's so hot," Amy replied.

"I'll change into something cooler."

Amy looked at him as he stood at the adjoining door, then said quietly, "If only I hadn't forgotten my hat."

In his own room, Edward changed quickly, regretting his pedantic use of cuff-links, and decided to wear blazer and flannels. It was a conservative choice and he knew it, but he felt at ease in such clothes. Amy had once remarked that they suited him, that she liked them more than anything else, and so that was what he chose. A navy blue blazer (mercifully without a badge) with flapless pockets, grey flannels, white shirt, cravat if desired. If one ever had the opportunity to peruse the Lytton album, holiday snaps gummed above coy captions, one would see Edward dressed like this before innumerable tourists' joys. There is one particular favourite, taken, it appears, before or below Milan Station; Edward and Amy standing side by side, the former smiling into camera, the latter looking to her left at something we cannot see that has caught her attention. In most of the others, however (Amy behind the lens), Edward is alone.

As Edward was exchanging his shoes for a lighter pair, he saw Amy's shadow through the partition door. She was standing up, and he could see from the silhouette that she appeared to be naked—but this may have been not quite the case. Her arms were above her head as if she were stretching, attempting to reach the ceiling (the shadow, in contrast, was seeking to penetrate Edward's room), and then the arms were lowered and the body angled to reveal the outline of breasts on the carpet. Edward stared at the shape like a child, tom-peeping into a lighted window, and leant forward, angling his body so that he could now see the waist, bottom, thighs. Then suddenly the shadow was pulled away from his sight, and he heard a wardrobe door being opened, a rattle of metal hangers, and then it was closed.

After ten minutes Amy was ready and stood on the balcony as Edward leafed through a tourist guide, a gift from the management. It offered little for the aesthete (primitive art, the dubious presence of an anchor belonging to Columbus in the National Museum), encouraging visits to the Casino instead or perhaps, of course, the market in Kenscoff.

"There's always the Citadel," Edward said, "but that takes a whole day at least. One has to go there by plane and then by mule."

Amy made no reaction. She was now wearing a favourite white dress, her hair loose.

"What's the matter?" Edward asked.

"I don't know. Nothing."

"It was your idea to come to Haiti."

"It's not that."

A pause, then Edward stood up and walked across the room and stood near her, not looking at her but at the view beyond. He was silent for a moment, then he said tentatively:

"We must forget it ever happened."

It was finally decided that they should visit Kenscoff, as if there had been any doubt in Edward's mind.

"I was told it was worth visiting," he said, but didn't elaborate.

He was now standing in the doorway of the hotel, waiting near a taxi while Amy posted her letters to England. It was still hot, but guests were now appearing from their rooms and walking towards the pool or driving into the town. A few of the more traditional English visitors were sitting on the terrace in a group of two or three, talking very quietly, elbows off the table, while taking tea and cakes, served by black waiters in white bow-ties.

"Hello again."

A woman's voice was heard just behind Edward, and he turned and saw the girl with red hair (Alice) walking up the driveway.

"Aren't you hot?" she asked. "Dressed like that."

"No," Edward replied. "Not yet."

"God, *I* would be hot."

"Did you find out about the bank?"

"What?"

"The bank. You said you were—"

"Oh yes. No. I don't think there is one. Never mind. Good-bye."

He watched as the girl walked towards the hotel steps, and then as she reached them she stopped suddenly, as if seeing someone she recognized. She had raised her hand in a form of greeting and then held it

59   The *Houngan*

back, unsure. It was then that Edward saw Amy. She was coming down the steps (two short flights at an angle to each other) and had reached the central platform, when Alice stopped and appeared to say something to her. The words, naturally, were inaudible, but Edward saw his wife shake her head then continue her descent past the redhead and down onto the gravel, walking away from the hotel without looking back. Behind her, Alice stared at her, a look of puzzlement, then shrugged and entered the hotel.

"She thought I was somebody else," Amy explained as they sat in the taxi. "Somebody she had met before."

Edward watched the hotel as the car circled before it, the driver honking the horn to disturb a dog. The terrace slid into view, the white balustrade, and he saw Lapôtre leaning on a cane, his back to them, and then the redhead sitting on a chair lighting a cigarette. He studied her, swivelling his head around slowly as the car accelerated, and then, just as she was about to disappear from sight, he saw her raise her head, a drift of smoke, as a man emerged from the shade of the terrace and stood next to her. A striped canopy, however, eclipsed the upper half of his body, so that it was impossible to recognize who he may be, or even whether he was white or black.

"Like the people last week," Edward said, turning around. "They mistook you for somebody else as well."

"What people?"

"At the barbecue on the beach. They thought they had seen you swimming in the sea."

Amy looked up sharply.

"Well obviously they were wrong."

Edward didn't answer but stared consciously ahead of him. The taxi had stopped at the end of the driveway to allow a column of small schoolchildren in white starched shirts, hands holding hands, to pass from left to right. They were following a teacher and were chanting, in chorus, a form of nursery rhyme.

"Edward," Amy continued, her voice rising. "You didn't believe them, did you?"

"Of course not. You can't swim, Amy. You told me that many times."

There was a hesitation and Amy glanced at the driver, then said quietly but emphatically, "The girl made a mistake. It happens all the time. If you don't believe me, ask her."

"Oh, don't be silly, Amy," Edward replied, lowering the window to let in some air.

It was a gentle rebuff on Edward's part and that really would have been the end of it. They would have visited what they wanted to see and then gone home to England, and everything would have been forgotten. The minor incidents, voices, appearances, and confusions would have been seen as petty phobias to be embellished into separate anecdotes to entertain a friend or two as wine glasses were refilled yet again.

But it wasn't the end and in a sense Edward knew it, for within two hours Daniel Azevedo had stepped from the periphery and had entered their lives, both Edward's and Amy's, and from that moment, the tragedy—for this surely was what it was—took hold of them all. One by one.

5 If seen from a height, from a tall building say, or an adjacent hill, the Marché du Fer appears like an orderly series of rectangles and squares, one-story buildings decorated in iron curlicues and clock towers and pillars that stretch from the slums of the waterfront to the edge of the Presidential garden and no farther. A mile perhaps, if one ever considered walking its length, though that is rare; not because of the heat or the distance (daunting enough in alien streets) but because each yard of the journey would be impeded by stalls and beggars and touts, hands reaching out, and the road would be blocked by merchandise, baskets, low tables, and people. It was the latter the Lyttons noticed first, not only the number but the colour, surprising them. This blackness. Taken away from the sanctuary of the hotel and the pale faces of European and American, they had been unprepared for what they now saw, absurd as it may seem.

At first, they tried to accept it rationally, to say to themselves that it was a Black Republic and so naturally the people were black; but then, as each corner passed by to reveal yet another street, another crowd, they began to be nervous, to sweat and seek shelter in one of the covered markets, pushing past fingers and shouts and stepping into the darkness of a building the size and shape of a terminus. They would then relax, move closer to each other, only to find that they were surrounded by alleyways no wider than a high-backed chair, and running between tables laden with mangoes and pannets of rice and carved-mahogany ornaments, and that they were in a maze, leaving a second beggar only to encounter a first, and that their only escape was towards the light and into the street, pushing and elbowing once more and clutching to each other's arm.

The plan, in fact, had been simple when outlined in the security of the taxi, side by side. They would make a detour to buy a film for Edward's Kodak (the driver had knowledge of a shop), present another film to be printed, and then continue to their destination, camera ready for the requisite snap.

"The driver says that there is a photographer's in the Iron Market," Edward had explained. "It doesn't *sell* iron, Amy. That is what it is made of."

It resembled a series of Parisian railway stations, not unlike the Gare du Nord, and from a distance seemed to be of interest. It was only when they left the taxi, and were told that they could only reach the shop by walking, that they regretted this departure from their plans. The driver himself had refused to accompany them, saying, that he would wait for them but that was all. Edward repeated this to Amy.

"Oh, I don't mind at all," she said.

"Are you sure?"

"Yes."

The journey took them half an hour, and when they returned the driver was nowhere to be seen. Immediately, Edward looked around, attempting to assess where they were, fearing they had made a mistake. "It must be the other corner," he said.

"No."

"What? How do you know?"

"I remember that sign. And the taxi is still here."

Amy pointed towards the car, now covered in children who were sitting on the bonnet and on the roof and were staring at them.

"Then where is he?"

63 The *Houngan*

"I don't know."
"Oh God, Amy, we can't stand here."
"Perhaps you ought to look for him."
"But where?"
"Did he say he would wait here?"
"Yes. I told you."
"All right. Then he must come back."
"Is that all you can say?"
"*You* wanted to buy the film, Edward."
"Oh for Christ's sake, we can't just stand *here*."

It is said that on certain days up to ten thousand Haitians visit the Iron Market. The majority come from Port-au-Prince itself, but there are some who come from as far away as Saint-Marc or even the island of Tortuga. When the writer Hesketh Prichard visited Haiti in the nineteenth century, when it was a country of Generals, he described a slaughter in the market place, a man struck down by an ironshod club of cocomaque. *A bleeding figure in the road* he wrote for the Victorian palate, *and the blazing sun over all.* No one has cared to read the book since those salad days, but Edward had, drawing it from his esoteric library in Bond Street and reading it during a lunch-break. The baroque images had remained in his mind, awaiting the occasion.

"We ought to get out of here," he said, retreating to a wall.
"But where to?"
"I don't know. If we keep walking, we're bound to find another taxi."
"But in which direction?"

Edward stared around him, attempting a display of confidence, and assessed the streets. They all appeared to be the same, no landmarks glimpsed between buildings to indicate a haven. *Why,* he thought, *am I always lost?* Even as a child he had been brought home by a neighbour more than once, found clutching a copy of *Wizard* and wandering aimlessly within a stone's throw of his own house.

"It's a game," Edward said in despair. "Someone's playing a game."

The *houngan* found them ten minutes later. He had been sitting on the back of a *tap-tap,* sitting cross-legged on the tail-board of the jitney and had seen the crowd, and then beyond them the pair of white faces, each looking in opposite directions. He had recognized Edward immediately, understood the situation, and had walked towards them across the street, parents pulling children aside, granting him a corridor to the steps and then to the boardwalk itself. It was a gesture of respect by those around him, a tacit stepping aside reserved for the priests of both the country's religions, as well as, though with less grace, for the *tonton macoutes*. Indeed, there was nothing to distinguish the *houngan* in his appearance from any other man, for he wore a striped Miami shirt outside cotton trousers, just as they did, had his hair cropped close to the head as they did, and was as clean-shaven as they were. He wore no jewellery, no watch or rings, or even an amulet around his neck; he was simply, to the white outsider, another face in the crowd. His name, Jean-Dantor.

"Hello."

Edward didn't recognize him at first, thinking him to be the taxi-driver, startled to find the man suddenly standing before him.

"Can I be of help?"

The English was naturally spoken with an accent and often abandoned in despair for the native language. Such a bilingual attempt on the part of the writer, however, will be avoided. It is needlessly tedious, this verbal pit-a-pat, though the reader may be assured that what follows is accurate, not only in sense but in mood.

"My name is Jean-Dantor. We have met before."

"Yes," Edward said, suddenly realizing who the man was, avoiding Amy's gaze. Nearby, a woman in a red dress, a crucifix around her neck, was placing panniers in a row filled with melons and other fruit. It was now ten minutes past five.

Jean-Dantor studied Edward, his head on an angle, his eyes slightly opaque, then turned his gaze on Amy.

"This is my wife," Edward stammered, gesturing towards Amy—as if there was any doubt that he could be referring to anyone else. "My wife, Amy."

Jean-Dantor made no reaction, but continued looking at Amy as if seeing something unexpected, almost sinister, like a doctor who is hiding an unhappy secret from a patient. The interpretation might be false, for immediately Jean-Dantor smiled—a row of white teeth, two of them capped in gold—and bowed, keeping his hands to his side.

"You have been shopping, Mrs. Lytton?" he asked.

"Yes," Amy replied shyly. "We are waiting for our taxi-driver but he hasn't come back."

"Hasn't come back? But he will come back. Is that his taxi?"

"Yes."

"Then he will come back."

"It has been a long time," Edward said.

"You must forget about time here, Mr. Lytton. We all live forever."

The expectation of life in Haiti is forty years, Edward repeated to himself. The fool had read that too.

"We will wait in the bar," Jean-Dantor continued. "Your driver will find us there."

Then, with another smile, he turned and walked along the boardwalk, stopping only to accept a melon from a small child, holding it and then returning it.

Edward and Amy didn't move, unsure of what to do, then followed, aware of the curiosity from those around them.

"Who is he?" Amy whispered.

"I can't tell you now."

"Tell me."

Edward glanced around, then said quickly, "The *houngan*," and walked on, pink-faced.

"The *what*?"

"Sshhh."

"I didn't hear you. What did you say?"

"The *houngan*, Amy. I don't want to say it too loud."

A look of almost infantile excitement suddenly appeared on Amy's face, the eyes widening, the mouth slightly parted as she looked up at her husband, the sun erasing all shadows.

"The *houngan*?" she repeated.

She looked like a child.

They were now sitting in the Bar itself, a metal table between them at the door. Three beers had been ordered, and then a pink beverage that was a particular favourite. Jean-Dantor had his back to the street, one arm resting along the top of a chair; opposite him, Edward and Amy, the latter leaning forward, her eyes not leaving the Negro's face. Behind them a row of stools, a barman mixing a cocktail, four or five youths huddled around a jukebox listening to American Rock. On the walls advertisements for Coca-Cola and Heineken, and above it a fan suspended from the ceiling. Apart from the persistent portrait of a late Duvalier, it was, therefore, like any bar in any town.

"I just didn't, well, expect to see someone like you walking around. No, that sounds silly."

It is of course Amy talking. Edward himself is saying little, looking as uncomfortable as he feels, an expression of apology on his face for his wife's behaviour. It is not necessary, for Jean-Dantor shows no reluctance to converse.

"Someone like me?"

"Well, what you are. Edward says you are a—"

"A *houngan*? Yes. But do you expect me to be ashamed of that, Mrs. Lytton?"

"No. Oh, no."

"Priests in England walk around the streets, do they not? They eat, sleep, talk, just like anyone else?"

"Yes, of course, but—"

"But I am different?"

"No. It's just that I thought voodoo was secret."

"Some. Not all."

"Do you mean it's legal?"

"Why yes."

"I didn't know that."

"Now you do, Mrs. Lytton."

"But what exactly do you *do*? Please tell me."

"I am a priest," Jean-Dantor said. "What do priests do?"

"They . . . perform a Mass."

"As I do."

67 The *Houngan*

"They worship God."

"We have many gods. Some we worship, some we do not."

"Like angels and devils?"

"If you wish."

Amy smiled, her face slightly flushed, and glanced at Edward, then gulped at her drink and said, "Do you . . . ?"

"What?"

"What I read?"

"What did you read?"

"You know . . . ?"

A hesitation, then Amy said quickly, "Cut off chickens' heads."

There was a sudden laugh and Jean-Dantor replied, "Yes. And other animals' too."

"Really?"

A shiver. Behind the Lyttons, three of the men at the jukebox had moved closer and were watching. It is doubtful whether they understood, but they were aware of the mood as once or twice Jean-Dantor glanced at them, a slight smile. Neither of the onlookers returned the smile but merely folded their arms and observed.

"Your gods are called *leahs,* aren't they?" Amy asked.

"Amy—please," Edward said nervously.

"You don't mind, do you?" Amy said to the *houngan.* "No."

"Then I am right?"

"They are called *loas,* Mrs. Lytton. *L-O-A.*"

"And you cut off chickens' heads to them? Bite their necks?"

Edward closed his eyes and looked away.

"It is much more complicated than that. But it is a sacrifice. Just like *your* priests, Mr. Lytton."

Edward suddenly realized he was being addressed: "What?"

"You are a Catholic, are you not?"

"Well, I—"

"You went to Mass this morning."

"How did you know that?"

"And your priest sacrifices to God, does he not?"

"Well, not chickens."

"No. Not chickens," Jean-Dantor replied and repeated this in French, glancing at the other men. The jukebox was now silent, the only sound being from the overhead fan but now and again voices from the street as the door was opened. Amy did not appear to notice that she was the centre of attention, and, if she did, it did not inhibit her. After all, they might easily have been discussing the state of the weather or the architecture of a countryhouse, three people exchanging views in the nicest possible way. ("Don't be fooled by Jean-Dantor," Edward warned the next day. "He is not as superficial as he appears." Amy had laughed, accusing Edward of being melodramatic. And who of us could blame her, sitting as she was now, across a table, drinking beer on a sunlit day like this?)

They remained in the Bar another five minutes before the driver arrived, much to Edward's relief. The conversation had now centred on the Church, that traditional target, and Edward resented it. He felt out of his depth, protesting that his belief was one of Faith and that it was impossible to argue that "on a logical basis."

"But my belief is the same," Jean-Dantor said, his voice remaining quiet and detached. "You see, you and I are similar."

"I can't see why."

"We both believe in an after-life, do we not?"

"Yes."

"Both believe that when we die it is not the end. Far from it."

"Yes."

"Both believe we must appease God."

"Well, yes . . . "

"Yes or no?"

"Yes, but there are differences."

"On the surface, of course. In your ceremonies you stand up and sit down. In ours—we dance."

"I think you are making fun of it," Edward said nervously, his skin reddening.

"Now why would you think that, Mr. Lytton?"

"I don't know— Look, we really ought to go and see if the driver has arrived."

"Do you think I'm making fun, Mrs. Lytton?" Jean-Dantor asked, turning to Amy.

"I don't know."

Jean-Dantor stared at her, inhaling deeply on a clay pipe. The expression of concern appeared on his face again, then he closed his eyes and remained like that for some time. Edward and Amy didn't move, not looking at each other, uncertain what to do.

"Do you believe you have a soul, Mr. Lytton?"

It was Jean-Dantor speaking, though his eyes remained closed, the voice almost inaudible. The mood had suddenly changed and Edward shuddered, though behind him nothing appeared to be different. Someone was laughing, leaning against the bar.

"Yes, of course I do," Edward replied.

"And when you die your soul must not be in a state of mortal sin. Is that not correct?"

"Yes. . . ."

"Otherwise you go to Hell. Is that not correct also?"

"It depends."

"On receiving Extreme Unction, you mean?"

"Yes."

"And if you do not, and you are in sin?"

"I believe we go to Hell."

"And if you die prematurely?"

"Prematurely?"

"By accident, for example. Before Extreme Unction can be administered?"

"I believe we go to Purgatory."

"And what is Purgatory?"

"A waiting."

"A waiting. And how will this waiting come to an end?"

"I believe by prayer."

"And during that waiting, will that soul return to earth?"

"No, of course not."

"We believe it does. We believe that the man who dies in an accident returns condemned to haunt the earth until his soul can be put to rest. Only then will he be at peace. Sometimes he will demand the death of someone else, someone he will choose. A loved one perhaps who has abandoned him. It is what Baron Samedi demands."

"We don't believe in that," Edward said.

"You think it hysterical nonsense? Black man's superstition?"

"I did not say that."

"No. But you thought it."

"I just don't believe the dead can return. I don't believe they can take on their mortal shapes and return."

"You don't believe because your Church says so."

"It is not that."

Blanche

"Then what is it?"

Full of dainty hungers.

"I just don't accept that they exist."

"Who exist?"

"*They* exist. You know what I mean."

"Tell me what I mean."

"They."

"Who's they?"

"*They.*"

"They?"

"They. Ghosts. Isn't *that* what you mean?"

"Yes," the *houngan* said finally. "I suppose that is what I mean. Ghosts."

Jean-Dantor leant forward and then repeated "Ghosts" once again and looked over the Lyttons' shoulders almost in a trance, staring at something or someone in the far corner. Slowly Edward turned, conscious that Amy also was moving her head around, so that all three people were now gazing in the same direction. In the corner, the light was almost nonexistent except for a narrow beam, green in colour that shimmered, jumped—a reflection from a bottle abandoned on the counter. The light, no larger than an acacia leaf, trembled on the eyes of a man who was standing very still, watching them. He had not been in the bar earlier but had just, so it appeared, arrived.

"There, you see, Mr. Lytton," Jean-Dantor said. "I told you your driver would find you here."

6 *Dear Mama,*
Dear mama dear mama dear mama dear mama dear mama dear mama. Please look after Cal for me dear mama. He doesn't really mean to chase the sheep dear mama.
Don't cry for me dear Mama
Blanche

It was cooler now, the heat rising from the dust of the street, the shadows darker, black merging into black. After leaving the Bar, the Lyttons had considered whether to abandon their plans to go to Kenscoff and return to the hotel. Edward believed that it might be too late but he was reassured that, on the contrary, it was the best of times.

"Then we will go," Edward said.

Amy agreed, saying that she would like to buy an English newspaper if it was possible, even if it was just to see the temperature in London. The driver pointed to a news agent across the street, and Edward watched as Amy, more relaxed now, made her way past the stalls to the pillared cloisters opposite.

"I must buy you a hat," he called out after her, and Amy turned, hearing but not understanding, and waited for Edward to repeat what he had said.

"I said I must buy you a hat," and gestured to the top of his head. "A hat."

Amy stared at him, then suddenly smiled and nodded and then was no longer there as an orange-and-blue *tap-tap* drove in front of her, hiding her from sight. When it had passed, she was standing by the news agent and peering at magazines.

"Your wife is at home here," the *houngan* said, moving beside Edward.

"Yes."

"But she has not been here before?"

"No."

"And how long will you stay?"

"Ten days more."

"Ten days? That is not long."

Edward didn't reply. Jean-Dantor sighed.

"We must talk again," he said.

"Perhaps."

"And your wife is called Amy?"

"Yes. I told you."

"Amy."

The word was said with quiet emphasis as if the *houngan* had just discovered it carved in stone, had brushed aside some moss with his fingers and found the name revealed. *Amy.*

The town of Kenscoff is six thousand feet above and to the south of the capital, set amid low mountains and surrounded by pines and shrubs of bougainvillaea and croton and fuchsia, the flowers of the last being the size and colour of a watermelon, and some, it is said, even larger. At night, if there is no wind and if the rain has fallen, the air is opaque with the fragrance of the flowers, so that visitors will travel perhaps fifty or sixty miles just to stand amid long grass and stare at the sky before returning to the car, stopping only to select a fuchsia as a memento to float in a bowl.

As Edward and Amy were being driven towards the hill, however, it was not yet dark or even dusk as they sat and gazed out of their respective windows, now and then pointing out a villa or a garden to each other, or a shrine erected by cross-roads. The road itself was narrow and uneven, turning back on itself on the edges of steep cliffs, so that a passenger would at one moment be gazing at a wall of rock close enough to the window to reflect his own image, and then suddenly he would be staring at sky, clouds, and would look down to see the road he had just travelled below him and the one he was about to enter directly above. There were no barriers between vehicle and space, no walls to offer protection; passengers were simply in the hands of the driver and no more.

"Are you nervous?" Edward asked as the car accelerated.

"No."

In time, the journey became monotonous—as it inevitably does when splendours become commonplace. We grow bored, our attention wanders as yet another miracle is held up for inspection, and we seek out mundane matters, finding amusement in trivia, enchanted by a mere pebble on the steps of the Acropolis.

"It reminds me a little of Norway," Edward said, dismissing the view. "There is even snow on the mountains. Do you see?"

"Where? Oh yes."

Amy raised her head from the newspaper (*The Times*, three days old), acknowledged the snow, then returned to an article on Etiquette.

"The fuchsias are nice," Edward then said to himself and recrossed his legs, making himself more comfortable. To his left a hawk hovered, dropped a few feet, then hovered again. Over the car engine could be heard the sound of large insects.

"What did you think of the *houngan*?" Edward asked finally.

"Who?"

"The *houngan*. Jean-Whatsisname."

"He wasn't as frightening as I thought he might be."

"Pretty frightening though."

"No. . . ."

"Oh, come on, Amy. He was a bit. All that nonsense he was saying."

"I just didn't think he was frightening."

"Well, he was being polite."

"How do you mean?"

"He was being polite, Amy. You asking him all those questions about chickens and things."

"I just wanted to know, that's all."

"There's more to it than what he said."

"I just wanted to ask."

A long silence. Edward stared at the driver's neck then said, "Amy?"

"Oh, Edward, I'm trying to read."

"Do you want to go back to England?"

"We will, next week."

"No, I mean now."

"Now?"

"Yes. Tomorrow, say."

Amy looked at him, puzzled, then said, "Of course not. Besides, it's raining there."

Edward thought about that for a while, his eyebrows set in a frown. Then he decided to say nothing whatsoever and just watch the road ahead. At one point, as the car turned yet another corner, he saw a field of corn set out below, a rectangle of saffron in a marquetry of green. He could see a man standing in the centre, standing very still, as if placed there in anticipation of crows. Naturally, it was Edward standing there, and he watched his alter ego, watched that wretched creature running towards the sanctuary of the road carrying in his mind base images that had haunted his dreams ever since, recurring incessantly between sleeping and waking. The man on his back, the woman in genuflection, *the movement of a metronome*. The nakedness of them both.

"There's a report here about that plane," Amy said.

Last night, the man had been Edward himself. He had felt earth under his back. In his bed, within sheets, he had felt the sensation of earth on the moist skin of his back, had felt the heat and the tremour of liquid. The sun had been blinding his eyes, so that he couldn't see the woman's face and had wanted her to lift her head so that he could identify her but her hair was falling over her face, curtaining her eyes and nose and brushing against his legs.

"That plane the captain told us about."

Then suddenly the woman had snapped her head away from him, hair smeared to mouth, as he felt his body catapult upwards, and he saw that it was, of course, Blanche. She was wearing a blue gingham dress and sitting on a swing in an orchard and reading a book. There was blossom on the trees so it was probably May or perhaps the beginning of June.

"What captain?"

"On the boat, Edward. You remember, he told us about the plane that crashed into one of the volcanoes at Revenants."

"What about it?"

"There's something about it in *The Times*."

Edward looked at Amy then at the newspaper.

"Why should it be in there?"

"It's only a couple of lines. I suppose they reported it because the woman was English. The man wasn't, but the woman was. It doesn't give their names."

"Perhaps they haven't informed the relatives yet."

"Yes. That must be why."

"Anything else in the paper?"

"Not much," Amy said. "Ulster and the Middle East and things like that. Even the letters are dull."

She then folded up the newspaper and threw it onto the seat.

"Waste of a dollar," she said.

It was the ambulance they saw first. The taxi had been reduced to first gear for about a mile, tires sliding on rock when it had suddenly braked, disturbing the Lyttons from their dreams, and then stopped altogether.

"*Qu'est-ce qu'il-y-a?*" Edward asked, leaning forward.

The driver pointed ahead and they saw the ambulance (a converted Dodge), another truck, and a group of people clustering at the edge of the road and staring at something Edward couldn't see. Behind the crowd were two mules, and behind them, four men who appeared to be running up and down without the slightest idea of what to do, since they were bumping into each other and shouting at the top of their voices. One of them held a rope and was trying to attach it to a mule. A small girl in red ribbons was being held up on the shoulders of a parent and was laughing.

"*Un accident,*" the driver said.

"God, what happened?"

The driver raised his right hand, fingers together, and moved it slowly upwards, then suddenly dipped the fingers and brought his hand down quickly towards the seat, like a child playing Spitfires, at the same time mouthing a guttural accompaniment culminating in a loud "*Voo-ooomp!*" He then switched off the car engine, took a copy of *Le Nouvelliste* from above the dashboard, and lit a cigarette as if such incidents happened all the time.

"It's an accident, Amy," Edward said.

"Let's go see," she replied immediately, opening the door, then adding as an afterthought, "We might be able to help."

They walked slowly, one behind the other, walking in the centre of the road. They could see the skidmarks parallel with the road for about fifty feet, then banking gently to the right, into and away from the truck, then disappearing under the feet of the onlookers before continuing towards the edge. A man in a pink shirt was pacing the length of each scar and writing the addition down in a small book.

At the rim of the road, Edward and Amy stopped, hesitated for a second, then looked down. The car, a Jaguar painted in a pleasant shade of blue not unlike the colour of certain matchboxes, was lying on its side thirty yards below, its grille embedded around the trunk of a pine tree. Surprisingly the distance was deceptive, for even from this height they could see the number plates (New York blue-and-gold), the Disneyland sticker on the trunk, and even hear the music from the tape-cassette ("Humoresque") that was still playing despite it all. Since it was a sports car, the observer was also privileged to notice the colour of the seats and the design of the dashboard, though the latter was now partially hidden by the rear of the hood that had somehow collapsed and retreated onto the upholstery as well as into the body of a woman who was lying backwards and staring up at the sightseers, her legs and arms jigsawed out of shape. She appeared to be laughing, but that was naturally an illusion for she was dead.

Edward gasped and wanted to look away but he couldn't, feeling compelled to stare at the horror below him, wanting absurdly to run down and switch off the music that had obscenely switched to a Sing-Along medley, an audience clapping hands. But he didn't move, glancing finally at Amy next to him and being startled to see that she was staring at the wreckage with an expression of rapt fascination, eyes wide, abstractedly chewing at a corner of her hair. It was as though she were a young girl, dressed in her best frock, watching a pantomime for the first time.

Edward looked away and became conscious of the noise behind him as a police car arrived; doors were opened, three men wearing dark glasses got out and glanced idly at the Jaguar. Then walked across to the ambulance and stood, hands on hips, talking to the truck-driver. It was clear that the car had swerved to avoid the truck, had failed, and had then bounced over the edge, cutting through two of three small trees (a branch was now lying on the pleated skirt of the dead girl) before being halted in its flight by the pine. It was also clear that there had been another occupant in the car, a man, who was now being collected from beneath a bougainvillaea and placed on a stretcher. He was not dead but he was dying.

"*Fou*," somebody said. "*Il est fou!*"

Moving away from the edge, Edward walked slowly across the road and pressed himself against the safety of the rock wall. He felt he ought to be sick but that was impossible. He just felt numb.

"*Monsieur?*"

Edward turned his head and looked down at an old man, yellow eyes gazing up at him. The Negro had his hand thrust forward, palm up.

"*Monsieur, je suis pauvre.*"

The hand was pushed farther forward and Edward stared at the face, the lines, the pitiful sadness. *Even here,* he thought, *there are beggars.*

"*Monsieur, je suis pauvre.*"

Edward shook his head and pushed the Negro aside and walked away. Then he stopped, his hand reaching into his pocket, and took out some coins.

"*Un moment,*" he called out, but the beggar was no longer there. He looked around and saw the old man lying on the ground by the truck. One of the policemen was standing over him and was raising a truncheon over his head. A second policeman walked by, kicked the beggar twice in the head, then walked towards Edward, smiled and said, "Okay?" then immediately retreated quickly back to the beggar and began to kick him again. Edward saw blood suddenly running under the wheels of the truck.

"Let's go," Edward said, taking Amy's arm. "Let us get out of here."

But Amy didn't move.

"Amy, for God sakes, let's go."

"They were staying in the hotel, weren't they?" she said, staring at the body of the man that was now being covered by a blanket.

"Yes," Edward said. "They're Americans. The man was playing the piano at lunchtime. I think his name was Borden. I don't know what the girl was called."

"It could have been us," Amy said.

They turned and began to walk back, Amy walking ahead. As she was pushing through the crowd, she suddenly stopped and looked down. Lying on the road was the girl's straw hat.

"Leave it," Edward said.

"It's just like the one I lost."

"Leave it, Amy," he repeated and took her arm and led her on towards the taxi, glancing back only to see that a small boy had picked up the hat and placed it on his head.

It was then, as they were walking past the truck, past the ambulance, that they saw Azevedo. He was standing alone, between them and the taxi, not looking at anything in particular but just waiting there as if he was passing the time of day. Edward hesitated, not knowing what to do, releasing his arm from Amy. But then Azevedo had seen him and was walking towards him.

"Did you see what happened, Edward?" he asked, not looking at Amy.

Edward shook his head. Azevedo nodded sadly and was silent for a moment, staring ahead of him at the revolving light of the ambulance. Then finally he said quietly, "It was me they were coming to see."

Part Three: Enemies

In the stumps of old trees with rotten hearts, where the rain/gathers and the laced leaves and the dead bird like a trap, there/are holes the length of a man's arm, and in every crevice of the/rotten wood grow weasel's eyes like molluscs, their lids open/and shut with the tide. But do not put your hand down to see, because

7 It was as if they had known each other from childhood, so that it seemed almost superfluous for introductions to be made. Nevertheless, they were, and Amy shook hands with Azevedo. A brief gesture, hand remaining in hand only for a moment before being released. Until that moment it had appeared to Edward that Azevedo had never really noticed that Amy was there. And vice versa. And yet as soon as Amy was introduced, Azevedo had turned towards her and smiled, not out of mere politeness, as may be expected, but almost out of recognition, as if he might say "Ah yes, you have had your hair cut differently" or "I really must return that book you lent me." This interpretation may be an exaggeration, and Edward had to admit that this might well be the case—since the accident had made him even more nervous than usual. That was to be understood.

Whatever Amy's feelings were, however, could not be discerned by any observer, even by Edward. She simply nodded hello and didn't move, looking at neither of the men as if waiting to be led. There was nothing, as Edward recalled later, to indicate how Azevedo's appearance affected her, neither favourably nor the opposite. He could have been a porter or a waiter, an impersonal and nameless presence that remains on the perimeter of one's day-to-day life. That, in retrospect, was the madness of it.

"I suppose there is nothing we can do," Edward said, looking towards the ambulance.

"No," Azevedo replied. "There is nothing we can do."

The three people then stood silently for a moment, each in their own entity, then finally Edward said, "I think it best if we go back to the hotel, Amy."

Edward had begun to walk towards the taxi when he heard Azevedo say, "I have a better idea. My villa is only half a mile away, just on the other side of this hill. It is not a palace but it will be a rest before driving all the way back."

Edward turned and looked at Azevedo. "No. . . . I think it best if we get back," he said.

"It is not far."

"No. Thank you but no."

Azevedo nodded and didn't move, watching as Amy walked towards her husband. It was then, even as she was walking, that Edward sensed something was wrong: for suddenly she faltered, began to gulp for breath, her hand raised as if trying to grasp at something for support, and then, slowly, she began to sink down, almost in slow motion, like a balloon coming to earth, her legs bending, angling slowly in front of her, her body bending backwards, the hem of the dress frozen for a second in mid-air, and then she was on the ground, edging into the dust and lying quite still. It had all happened in an instant, and Edward was calling out her name and running towards her, kneeling beside her.

"Amy!"

There was almost no movement and Edward glanced up and saw Azevedo watching, looking not at Edward but at Amy.

"Can you help me?" Edward called out.

"She has only fainted," Azevedo said, standing over her. "The heat. The accident. It is understandable."

"But what can we do?"

"She needs to lie down where it is cool. With cold water she will soon recover."

Edward stared at Amy anxiously, then suddenly stood up and ran to the ambulance, calling out to one of the attendants. He pointed back towards his wife: *"Ma femme . . . elle est . . ."*

He searched, scrambled frantically for the right word and repeated, *" Ma femme. Ma femme."* Then blurted out, *"Elle est malade."*

The attendant glanced casually along the road then shook his head. *"C'est impossible."*

"Mais elle est malade!"

"Tant pis."

Edward stared at him then immediately rushed towards the attendant, wanting to strike him, kick him like they had kicked the wretch of a beggar. But he didn't, even if he had had the courage to do so; for a man, blacker than most Haitians, suddenly stepped in front of him, and Edward knew even without being told that he was a member of that quaint body of avuncular thugs who are so much a part of the tourist trade. The Tonton rested one hand on the butt of an unholstered revolver at his belt, and said quietly, *"L'ambulance est occupée, monsieur."*

Edward stopped, feeling himself shaking, and stared at the Tonton and then at the covered stretchers that were being loaded into the ambulance.

"C'est occupée."

There was nothing more to say. Humiliated, Edward walked back to the unconscious Amy, then stared out across the valley, a river meandering at its base, the sea beyond that, and said without a blush, "Damn this *bloody* country."

It was in these circumstances that Edward and Amy visited Villa Azevedo for the first time, arriving there at sunset on their third day in Haiti.

Azevedo lived alone. Or at least so it appeared, since there was no one else to be seen, no houseboy or even a relative. It was just

Azevedo living in a villa that stood isolated, set amid a forest of pines, a two-story building that dated from the nineteenth century, somewhat Gothic in design. It was said to have been built for Jean-Pierre Boyer to be used as a hunting lodge, and indeed the interior reflected the late Napoleonic era, the years of Haitian Independence.

"Aren't you lonely here, all by yourself?" Edward asked as they stood in the library looking north towards Port-au-Prince.

"No," Azevedo replied. " I am used to it."

"Then you are Haitian?"

"Yes, of course."

Amy had regained consciousness since leaving the taxi and was now resting in a bedroom, lying on a carved mahogany bed similar to the one depicted by David to support and complement Juliette Récamier. Since her arrival, Amy had said nothing whatsoever and was believed to be asleep.

"But I thought all Haitians were black?" Edward asked.

"They are. But don't forget, this country was ruled by whites until the last century. Even under Dessalines, the French aristocracy held power. They were mulattoes of course, but they were white to everyone else. My father was a mulatto, my mother was French. In this country, that is the worst of both worlds. But it exists."

Edward was silent and Azevedo glanced at him.

"Does it make any difference? What I am?"

"No . . ."

"Because if it does, I would not be offended."

"No."

Azevedo smiled, sat down in a wing-backed chair, and studied a portrait on a wall. A woman, no more than twenty, dressed in a crinoline and holding a fan. In a corner of the painting were written the words: *Oui, mais c'est moi qui en souffre.*

"Thank you for your help with Amy," Edward said.

"Amy?"

"Amy. My wife."

Azevedo stared at Edward as if preoccupied with other matters, then said, "Ah yes. Your wife."

Silence. Azevedo suddenly seemed to retreat into the chair as though Edward didn't exist. Outside, the sky was scarlet and the lights from the city could be seen in the distance. Edward now felt as if he didn't belong, an intruder, and yet, not daring to move, waiting for the man in the chair to tell him to sit down or help himself to a drink. He thought about Amy and wondered whether he ought to go and see if she was better; but, even if she was, the taxi would not return for another hour—so they would have to stay till then. It was therefore for the best, he considered, if Amy remained alone; then they would leave and never return.

Careful not to make any sound, almost treading on tiptoes, he looked at the books on the shelves, mostly leatherbound tomes on topography, collections of Balzac and Dumas, *père et fils*. On another shelf, near a desk, were more modern books, in both French and English. Books of quotations and poetry, books by Butor and Böll and Borges (*Labyrinths* in English, French, and Spanish), a series of manuals on flying, a pilot's handbook, a portrait of Pushkin, half a dozen entertainments, some other novels. Edward selected one at random. It was called *Quelque Chose au Coeur*, a translation. On the opening page Edward read: "*Pour moi, il n'est pas d'histoire plus déplorable que celle-ci*. And on another page: *Elle avait décidé d'épargner mes sentiments à tout prix. Et elle se rendait bien compte que, à cette époque, la plus dure punition pour lui eut consisté à ne jamais revoir sa femme. . . . Je suppose que je vous ai exposé clairement la situation. J'en arrive à présent au 4 août 1913, mon dernier jour d'ignorance totale, et aussi, je vous l'affirme, mon dernier jour de bonheur parfait. Car la venue de la petite avait encore ajouté à ma béatitude.*" It was as Edward was reading this paragraph as best he could that he suddenly realized that Azevedo was talking to him.

"It was always you I wanted to visit me."

Perhaps he had been speaking for some time. Edward closed the book and placed it back on the shelf. Below it, on the desk, was a photograph frame. It was empty but whatever picture had once been inside had not been removed—merely reversed, hidden; for the Photographer's Stamp could be seen, the kind that is placed on the back of enlargements. It was in English.

"I'm sorry," Edward said, turning around. "What did you say?"

"I only asked those Americans because you refused."

"I had things to do."

"I didn't want them here. They weren't right."

"What do you mean?" Edward asked, puzzled.

Azevedo looked up, smiled, and said, "They wouldn't have liked it here, Edward. Not as you do. You and Amy."

Edward didn't reply. It seemed a curious thing for the man to say, and yet it was probably a compliment. Indeed, Edward considered it as such and was flattered. He had to admit that the villa was impressive, an anachronism in Haiti, and he had no regrets.

After checking on Amy's condition (she was asleep, hand resting upon hand upon waist), the two men played backgammon, a glass of wine on either side of the baize table. Edward had never played before (unlike Amy, he had not been a devotee of games, even at Christmas) and yet now he found he was enjoying learning, and even decided to purchase a backgammon set when he returned to England. Furthermore, he realized he liked the companionship as they talked of, oh, a hundred things, discussing with enthusiasm subjects that Edward would normally have avoided or been too shy to announce that they appealed to him. They talked about Edward's career, his Victorian Juvenilia that no one else had previously cared about. He found himself enthusing without embarrassment, without that pitiful stammer, about Crane and Greenaway and Caldecott and his favourite Chapbook (*Tommy Thumb's Songbook for All Little Masters and Misses*); it had all seemed so absurd and infantile before, a grown-up man doting on such things, but Azevedo never once made it appear so. He asked and he listened and he praised and Edward knew that he liked him; that he wanted him to be a friend. He had found, if you wish, an equal.

Later, Azevedo showed his guest the rest of the house, both men carrying full glasses of wine, and in one room (a third bedroom), Edward pointed to a chair and said, "You have Amy's hat."

"Where?"

"On that chair. That is my wife's hat."

Azevedo laughed and opened the door towards the stairs, while Edward hesitated, picked up the straw hat, then returned it to the chair.

"I could have sworn that was my wife's hat," Edward said, catching up with Azevedo. "But then there must be hundreds of hats like that."

"No. That one is unique," Azevedo said, and they walked into the garden to admire the hibiscus. It was dark outside, but there was light from the house casting negatives of windows on the lawn. They walked in silence, stopping now and again to stare at a shrub or a tree or a small statue. The insects continued.

"Do you have many guests here?" Edward asked, standing hands in pockets, the empty glass resting on a low wall.

"Not any more. Even if I asked them, they would be afraid to come."

Edward looked at him, but there was little elaboration.

"When Magloire was President my father would invite people here. Mostly white. Mostly foreign. Then in 1957, everything, of course, ended."

"Is your father alive?"

"No."

"And your mother?"

"My mother never came to Haiti. Not once. I was born in Europe. I didn't return here till Duvalier was in power. Not because I liked him. I didn't. It just seemed an act of cowardice to be anywhere else."

A silence, and Azevedo added, "And now I have enemies."

Then suddenly he broke the mood and smiled. "So you see, Edward, I really prefer to be alone."

"I am the same. Amy likes guests, visitors, but I would rather be alone as well. I have a shyness of people."

"I would never have known that."

"People embarrass me. I like them, but I never feel at my best with them. I want to be—I don't know—witty, relaxed. To be able to complete an anecdote without seeing that restlessness on the listener's face."

"It's your imagination, Edward."

"No. I know I just appear . . . well, 'ordinary.' Or even perhaps slightly absurd. I know that. I really don't think I'm memorable to anyone. Not even to Amy. I wanted to be, and when I was younger I thought if I drank a little. Do you know what I mean? Just a little, to make things easier. But it didn't work. I'd either get drunk and people would look at my glass and not at me—I always seemed to be refilling my glass. Or I would just insult everyone. I didn't mean to. I wanted to flatter them, wanted to be liked, and instead I found myself criticizing everyone in the room. And so in the end I just thought, Oh well, it won't work. It's no good. I really *am* ordinary. A little bit of a bore. And so I chose to be alone. Even sometimes without Amy."

Azevedo didn't say anything, but sat down on the wall and lit a cigarette. In the darkness, the two men side by side, it reminded Edward of a confessional box; at least, Azevedo induced the trust of a confessor. "He wouldn't rat on one," Edward said to himself.

"With women, of course," he continued, "it was unbearable. I was like a bashful child. Still am. I'd blush and stammer and say . . . Oh, it was pathetic. I once thought of becoming a priest just because of that. Some people do. A boy in our school did, I know. 'I can't go through life being like this,' he said. And so he renounced women altogether and went into a seminary. I said good-bye to him at Paddington Station. He wrote to me for a while, and then, well, I suppose he was far too busy. I met him again only once. We bumped into each other outside Selfridges and went for a cup of tea in a corner shop. It's now been pulled down. I hated it. He told me the most extraordinary things. He said he had conquered his fear of women. He said he conquered it because he now knew how evil they were. It had begun, this bitterness, during Mass, when he had to place the host in their mouth, staring down into their mouth. He described the saliva, the lipstick stains, the teeth-fillings. I remember looking at him—he had a comical face, round and fat which made it worse—and listening to him telling me about their confessions. The women's confessions. What they did to themselves. . . . I thought he was drunk but he couldn't have been. I never saw him again but he's still a priest—somewhere in England."

Edward stopped as if suddenly aware of where he was.

"I'm sorry," he said.

"Are *you* still frightened of women, Edward?"

"Do you mean like that priest?"

"Yes."

"Yes, I am. Though I'm not frightened of what they may do to me. I am frightened of what I may not be able to do to them. Does that sound—"

"Don't explain."

"I just wanted to—"

"You don't have to."

"I just wanted to say that that priest didn't influence my feelings. I'm sure he didn't mean to do that. . . ."

A pause, then Azevedo smiled and said, "But you married, Edward. There was one woman who didn't frighten you."

"*Two*. No. One. Well, there was another, but she's dead now."

They began to walk around an ornamental pond. Then, later, sitting on the terrace, the glasses refilled, Edward said, "The last book Rackham illustrated was *The Wind in the Willows*. He was very old then and confined to bed. They all knew he was dying. He had his easel propped up on his lap and his daughter—I think it was his daughter—told him to rest. Not to work. Because she knew he was dying. Rackham finally agreed and closed his eyes. Then suddenly he opened them and said, 'Ratty hasn't got any oars.' It was a picture of Rat and Mole by the river. It's rather pretty. A green-shuttered house and a blue boat. 'Ratty hasn't got any oars.' You see he had forgotten to draw them. So he did and then he died. It was the last thing Rackham ever said."

Edward smiled shyly. "Ratty hasn't got any oars. . . ."

Azevedo stood up and walked towards the door and into the house.

"*You* must have known many women?" Edward asked, aware of this boldness but not surprised by it.

"I only remember one," Azevedo replied.

"First love?"

"In a sense."

"What happened?"

"She left me."

"Left *you*?"

Two lights could be seen moving towards them, illuminating branches as they approached and then they stopped and went out.

"The taxi's returned," Azevedo said, almost with regret.

Amy still appeared to be asleep. Edward had called her, heard no answer, then went up the stairs to wake her. The bed was empty.

"Amy?"

He looked out of the window but couldn't see anything because of the darkness. It was obvious that Amy had recovered, for she had been reading a book while the two men were in the garden. It was now lying on the rumpled pillow, a page of the second chapter folded at the corner. Edward picked it up idly and read:

"*Ne vous inquietez pas de cela maintenant, Mr. Bendrix. Je demande trois guinées pour cette consultation préliminaire—*"

And then he placed the book down and opened an adjoining door, but it led only into an empty bathroom.

On the stairs he called out Amy's name again.

"Isn't she there?" Azevedo asked.

"No."

"Perhaps she has gone for a walk."

"In the dark—" Edward replied, and then said abruptly, "She doesn't speak French!"

"What?"

"The book she was reading. It was in French."

They decided to look for Amy in the house, visiting each room in turn. In the third bedroom, Edward said, "I'm sure that's Amy's hat."

She was found in the library, waiting as if she had been there all the time. Though she still looked pale, she assured them she was better and apologized for being ill.

"You must never apologize," Azevedo said. "You know that."

Amy smiled and said, "It must have been the heat."

As they walked towards the front of the villa, Azevedo touched Edward's arm and said in a whisper, "She probably just *reads* French. That's all. It is not uncommon."

Edward didn't reply but collected his camera from the table by the door and followed Amy out onto the lawn. "Thank you," Amy said turning towards Azevedo. She reached out her hand and seemed to touch him on the arm. "If I hadn't fainted I would never have seen your house."

"And you are not disappointed?"

"No."

The word was said quite quietly and without hesitation. "No." For a brief moment Edward felt once again as if he was an intruder, someone who has entered a room without knocking. Instinctively he found himself stepping out of the darkness into the light, moving closer to Amy, more protectively, and saying, "We didn't expect to see a house like this in Haiti. Did we, Amy?"

But Amy made no comment and looked up towards a lighted window.

"That's not the bedroom I was in, is it?"

"No," Azevedo replied.

"From there, from that bedroom, can you see the Caribbean?"

"Yes. Only from that window."

Amy nodded and then walked away.

"Good night, Mrs. Lytton," Azevedo called after her, but there was no reply. Amy simply stood staring up at the lighted window.

"Perhaps we will see each other again," Azevedo said, turning his attention to Edward. "That is if you don't have 'Things to do.' "

"No, nothing," Edward replied quickly and began to walk away when Azevedo took his arm and said quietly, "You will not tell anyone that you have seen me here, will you?"

Edward shook his head. No. It would be a secret between them. Then he smiled and walked towards the taxi that was parked a hundred yards away at a turning in the driveway. The driver was leaning on the hood smoking a cigarette.

"*Le Grand Hotel Dessalines, s'il vous plaît.*"

The driver gestured towards the villa. *"C'est vide?"*
"Vide?"
"Cette maison-là?"
"Non. Pas du tout."
The driver shrugged, and got into the car, and started the engine. Edward then glanced back and saw Amy. She was walking slowly towards him, and at that moment she appeared to Edward to be remarkably plain, almost unnaturally so. Plain and ultimately rather dull. As she reached him, the lights behind her on this side of the villa went out.

"I don't like that kind of man," she said.

In the taxi back towards Port-au-Prince, Edward was silent, sitting as far away from his wife as he could, allowing not even a sleeve or the corner of his blazer to touch her. Even when Amy spoke ("Blanche talked of a bedroom like that"), Edward didn't reply.

After some time, when Amy accepted that she was being ignored, Edward suddenly said quietly, though loud enough for Amy to hear, *"Tu es laide et une menteuse."*

There was no reaction. Edward studied his wife's face out of the corner of his eye, but there was not the remotest indication that, even if she had heard the insult, she had understood what it meant. She simply sat, hands together, and gazed ahead of her, almost as if she was daydreaming.

8 When the Lyttons arrived at the Dessalines two police jeeps were parked in the driveway, and guests and outsiders were standing silhouetted in the lights of the hotel.

"I wonder what's happened now?" Amy asked.

"How should *I* know?" Edward replied, and paid the driver before walking towards the main steps. As he reached the first flight, he looked up and saw Alice standing alone on the main terrace. There was a look of profound disappointment on her face, as if a long-desired dream had suddenly been scotched, taken away from her. Edward tried to attract her attention and even called out her name, but she either couldn't or wouldn't see him, remaining isolated by a carved white pillar, her red hair piled up on her head. Even to the most casual observer, she looked beautiful.

At the desk, Edward collected his keys, glanced back at the crowd, and asked, "Why are they here? The police?"

The desk-clerk sighed and said, "Two Americans were killed in a car crash."

"Which two Americans—?" Edward began, and then realized and said, "Oh yes. Of course."

He had forgotten so soon.

Moving away from the desk he found himself staring at a television screen that had been set up above the bar. A group of men, bored with real-life drama, were drinking beer and watching a replay of an old American movie, *Four Daughters,* subtitled in French.

"It's because of the car crash, Amy," Edward repeated, and turned around to find he was saying this to Lapôtre.

"I believe I saw your wife talking to Jean-Dantor."

"Who?"

On the television screen, John Garfield was sitting on a park bench looking up at a girl. It was a familiar image.

Edward found Amy outside sitting in a deserted tennis court. Next to her, the *houngan.*

"Amy?" Edward called out, pushing open the metal gate, walking across the grass towards them.

"We were talking about the accident," Amy said casually and smiled, rubbing the side of her face. "And ghosts and things like that. Like the two old ladies of Versailles."

Edward stared at her and glanced at Jean-Dantor, who was leaning back, eyes half-closed.

"I think-think we ought to go back, Amy," he said.

"Your wife is very receptive, Monsieur Lytton," the *houngan* murmured.

"I think we ought to go back to the hotel."

As if to demonstrate the statement, Edward turned and walked away, and then stopped when he heard Amy say:

"Tell me what you said about ghosts returning. The victims of an accident. Those Americans couldn't, surely."

Edward heard the *houngan* laugh and reply:

"Not to us. No. They were probably Baptists or whatever Yankees kneel for. Do the Baptists have ghosts? Or the Quakers?"

"Amy!" Edward interrupted. "Let's not begin this again. This nonsense."

"Sssh!" Amy said and leant closer to the *houngan,* looking up at him. "But *you* believe ghosts appear?"

"Yes. I believe in that. But if *you* don't, they don't exist. As Christ does not exist to me. Nor his mother or father. Whatever they are."

"Let us not get personal," said Edward loudly.

"Personal, Monsieur Lytton?"

"I didn't mean that. I mean I don't want to be God's advocate. We've been through that."

The *houngan* shrugged. Amy had found a tennis ball and was bouncing it on the ground, watching Edward.

"I suppose you think you are blessed with some kind of divine insight?" Edward said, approaching, but not too close.

"Yes. I have to believe that. I am."

"Catch!" Amy shouted, throwing the ball. It rolled unimpeded towards the net.

"Tell me about your ghosts," she said.

"It is too complicated. Besides, if it is just primitive superstition to you, I will not waste my time."

"But I want to know."

"Amy—I'm going to bed," Edward said, but didn't move.

"If these victims return," Amy continued, "how can one recognize them?"

"It is a rare case. As I said, it is only if someone has died prematurely, before receiving last rites, that the person returns."

"Prematurely? You mean an accident?"

"Perhaps."

"But that's not *rare*," Edward said defiantly. "Accidents simply are not rare."

"No," the *houngan* replied calmly, "but we are all given these rites as a child, often at birth. As a security, if you wish. There are few exceptions."

"Only Haitian?" Amy asked.

"No. There *are* whites who have adopted our religion. It is an aberration, but we have converts like anyone else."

"You are talking about voodoo?"

"What else?"

"And how does one recognize these ghosts?"

99 Enemies

"They seek you out. Often someone they love or want to be loved by."

"And then?"

"Then?"

"What happens then?"

"They die."

"Who dies?"

"The ones who have been chosen."

Edward, who had been silent, suddenly laughed, kicked the tennis ball, and said, "You mean they die of love for the ghosts? Oh, that is absurd."

"Why should it be absurd, Monsieur Lytton? Do you consider martyrs absurd? Obviously not, because your Popes canonize them."

"But they don't die for someone who is already dead."

"Don't they?"

Edward stared at the *houngan*. "No, I cannot accept that. It *is* just superstition."

"Your martyrs die for someone who is immortal in order to be immortal themselves, do they not?"

"In a sense, but these victims you are talking about are already dead."

"Not to us. Nor, indeed, to them."

Silence. Then Amy said, her eyes not leaving the *houngan*'s face, "These people who have been chosen—is there no way of stopping them from dying? From killing themselves, say?"

"Yes."

"How?"

"If the ghost is killed again. And given the last rites. It is the only way."

"Have you ever done that?"

"Yes."

"They are killed again?"

"Yes."

"Do they *bleed*?" Edward snapped.

Jean-Dantor smiled, then laughed.

"Do they?" Edward repeated.

"Monsieur Lytton, don't try and play the fool."

Edward blushed, walked away, hesitated, and said, "It's nonsense, isn't it? What you said?"

"To you, perhaps. But not to me."

"I'm going to bed. Amy?"

But Amy merely gazed across the tennis court in her own individual space, hand within hand on her lap.

"What are those lights?" Edward asked suddenly.

"Only the ambulance," the *houngan* replied.

Edward stared at the ground, then walked away before returning once more and saying, "I myself couldn't see a ghost, could I?"

"Could you see a vision?"

"That's different."

"Why?"

"I'm going to bed."

"Why is it different?"

"We're being esoteric."

"It's only different in that to you a vision is attributed to God. To us, a ghost is attributed to the devil."

"The devil?"

"Baron Samedi. He is our God of Death."

"But he's not *my* God. This Baron Saturday—Samedi."

"No. But he could be the ghost's."

"I'm going to bed."

This time, Edward continued walking until he was out of the court and on the path to the hotel. He glanced back and saw the *houngan* suddenly lean towards Amy and place his hand on her leg. Slowly Amy looked at him, then she was standing up and hurrying towards the gate, not stopping until she reached Edward. Her eyes appeared to be very bright, almost translucent.

"I just wanted to know," she said and walked beside him.

Though it was not yet nine o'clock, the Lyttons decided to retire early. It had been, as Edward wrote in his diary, a long and uneasy day.

"You didn't *really* believe what the *houngan* told you, did you?" Edward had asked as they approached the hotel.

"Blanche did."

"She told you that?"

"Yes."

"Oh, Amy, Blanche believed in all those things for a time. Buddhism and Indian mysticism and whatever. They were just games for her."

"That was before."

After this, husband and wife talked little as they sat in Edward's room before a folding table. Shutters had been closed against the mosquitoes and a trolley of food had been ordered and delivered, though neither of them felt hungry. A salad was picked at, but there was no appetite.

"He said he'd probably see us again," Edward remarked, almost to himself.

"Who? Jean-Dantor?"

"No. Daniel."

Amy flicked a glance across the table on hearing the prenomen and smiled.

"What are you smiling at?" Edward asked.

"Nothing."

"Well, that's his name, isn't it?"

Amy continued smiling, then as if trying to suppress it, placed her left hand across her mouth.

"I don't think it's funny," Edward said, almost with petulance.

"Does he call you 'Edward'?"

"Yes, of course."

The smile immediately collapsed into laughter and Amy was forced to look away, then gulp a glass of water. In doing so, she caught sight of Edward's expression (salmon-pink face, hurt outrage) and laughed again, muttered a token "I'm sorry," and stood up, turning her back to him, shoulders shaking.

"Amy—what's the matter with you?"

No answer.

"You ought to be very grateful to him. He looked after you."

Further laughter and Amy waved a hand helplessly in the air as if semaphoring a coda and hurried through the adjoining door into her room. Edward didn't move but sat staring at the space which his wife had just occupied. It was the heat, he thought. The accident. She was still not herself, poor thing.

Later, in the early hours, he heard his name being called once again.

He assumed it must have been about two o'clock in the morning. He hadn't slept, though he had put on his pyjamas and had gone to bed well before midnight. No further words had been exchanged between husband and wife, apart from a single good night, and Edward had lain in bed thinking of the day and listening to the sounds of the night. Amy worried him, not her physical health but her character. She had changed, he knew that, and as he explored the events of the holiday he began to feel nervous and very much alone. The dark, as we all know, is a dangerous companion for anxiety; it is deceptive, encouraging the worst of fears. Indigestion begets cancer, fidelity begets treachery, and an engaged tone can beget paranoia. We jump at shadows, curse forsaken resolutions, feel persecuted, unloved. It is all, of course, irrational if seen in the light of day, but this is a pathetic poultice when darkness still exists and imagination is an enemy. For Edward, however, it wasn't imagination, and, God knows, he wished it was. The behaviour of Amy was one thing, but the voices were another.

"Edward."

At first he thought it was Amy and had answered, but there had been no reply. And yet it sounded like Amy's voice.

"Edward."

But somehow the timbre was different. A woman's voice that was not quite Amy's, yet familiar. That was what made him sit up, eyes staring into the darkness. There was no interrogation in his name being called. No request for an answer. It was just stated simply as if in recognition. *Edward.*

He was now at the main door, for the voice seemed to come from the corridor outside as before. There was no doubt about that.

Nevertheless, he checked the adjacent room, pushing open the partition door quietly, a few inches, and saw the shape of Amy in bed and could hear the breathing of sleep.

"Ed-ward."

He was now frightened; and he knew it. He was not, to be fair, a coward (like most shy people he was, in fact, physically brave), and so he didn't return to his bed but opened the door and stepped out into the corridor. He knew that if he didn't find out the cause he would never sleep anyway, and, besides, there was probably a simple explanation. After all, somebody else in the hotel may well be called Edward. Edward Pinfold, perhaps.

The corridor was empty, lit only by moonlight. It was also silent. There was not a sound, no voice or echo. Nothing at all. Edward stood there, a dressing-gown now around his shoulders, and was about to return to his room when the footsteps suddenly ran towards him. He froze immediately, gasped in terror as the steps approached quickly, one by one, gathering in momentum, hurrying towards him. There was no one there. Nothing whatsoever. Not even a shape and yet the footsteps continued. He began to tremble, wanted to scream, call out, but he couldn't as the steps reached him, and he felt a sudden gust of cold air and they were past him and were gone. *Oh my God. Please help me, God.* Silence. *God!* There was nothing. He could hear his breathing, feel his lungs, but that was all. He even dared himself to turn around, and, as he did, the footsteps began again, and this time he called out but his voice was stifled. He tried to move away, to avoid the spectre that must be pursuing him and clung to the wall, dislodging a picture. Catching it, he absurdly attempted to replace it on its hook and, as he did so, he suddenly realized he had been a fool. There was no ghost. No footsteps. His imagination had betrayed him yet again. Because he could see what it was.

Elated, like a child, he ran down the corridor and saw the open window and felt the cold wind. That's what it was. A row of pictures hanging along the length of the wall—small, light, silly little pictures that lay in the direct line of a draught. The wind entered, lifted each one in turn, dropped it back, and moved on. A tap. Tap. Tap. That's all it was. A petty basis for a fear.

Suddenly, as Edward closed the window tight and saw the pictures settle back against the wall, he felt ridiculously happy, as if this discovery had exorcised all the doubts, fears, questions that had plagued him since the beginning of the holiday. It was, if you wish, as if his anguished prayer had been answered and he had been shown the truth, the mundane logic that he had overlooked in his fantasies. There was nothing to worry about. There never had been. It was going to be the happiest of times after all.

An hour later, Edward Lytton was found shivering with fear in the garden, huddled against a tree.

9

"Will you stay here all night? Dressed like that?"

He had heard his name being called yet again. Standing in the corridor, just as Edward had thought the nightmare was over, he had heard his name and the fear had returned. He sought to trace it, to identify the prankster (for that surely is what it was), walking along the corridor away from his room, stopping now and again to listen. There were other sounds, of course, to be recognized and dismissed (the night itself, the hotel, party-music from Alice's room), but the voice itself remained, fainter now, muffled, until finally it was no longer there.

"Your face is cut. Your feet, too."

He had been too terrified to return to his room. He had believed—there is no question about that; it was a belief, nothing less—had believed that he would open the door and see her hanging from the ceiling just as she had done before, the paisley scarf around her neck. And so he had run. Who could blame him for that?

"There is blood on your leg. It must be where you fell on the steps."

He had heard the piano too. Or was that going too far?

"Sit down. Sit down in here."

While Amy still snoozes, no doubt. And dreams.

"And dreams."

"What?"

"Sit down. Relax."

"Wha'ja just say?"

"There is nothing to be afraid of, Monsieur Lytton."

Edward allowed himself to be led onto the stone seat of a gazebo. He was aware of the moon in a clear sky, though not a full moon. That would be too artificial. Instead, a moon in parenthesis. Opposite him, his companion sat down and stared into space, as if the two men had just entered a public vehicle and were awaiting the initial jolt of motion before relaxing into conversation. Outside, chatter could be heard, music, though neither indicated the hour of the night, for Haiti is a sleepless country.

"Were you the one who was chasing me?" Edward asked finally.

"I was not chasing you," the *houngan* replied. "You were running away. I wondered why."

Edward stared at Jean-Dantor for a long time, then said, "I thought you were Blanche."

Above, unseen she stands naked against the shutter, watching. The mischief of fingers. Then she returns to her bed.

"Edward," she repeats to herself. As if in lament.

"Tell me about Blanche."

"I don't think I should tell you anything. It is difficult in English. It is even more difficult in French."

"Treat me as a stranger."

"You *are* a stranger."

"Then I will leave you. I wanted to be of help."

"Why?"

"Because you *need* help. You ran. You were frightened. *Are* frightened."

"But why *you*?"

"All right. Find someone else."

"I feel detached," Edward said suddenly. "As if I didn't exist. As if I am standing outside myself, looking at myself and saying, 'Who is that poor wretch sitting there in his pyjamas?' As if I was reading a book about someone called Edward Lytton who goes on holiday with his wife to Haiti, and I'm wondering what is going to happen next. I'm thinking, Oh dear, I've never met a chap like that. Chaps like that don't exist. Not any more. Do you understand?"

Jean-Dantor stood up and walked out into the darkness. For the first time, Edward looked at him, noticed his clothes (a form of burnous, more African than Haitian), then watched as the *houngan* moved into the shadows and was gone. He was alone once again. Turning his head he found himself looking at the small body of a bat. It was hanging from a shelf as if it had been thumbtacked there as a keepsake, its round fat stomach rising and falling. There were others.

It was daylight before Edward left the gazebo, and by that time some of the hotel guests were already going for an early morning swim. As he returned to the lobby he saw Alice. She was carrying a transistor radio, a book by Glyde, and a towel.

"Hello," she said and smiled.

You're beautiful, Edward thought. *Eyes, hair. Neck.*

"Good morning," he replied quickly, a sudden embarrassment at his appearance.

"Are you lost again?"

"In a way."

Alice smiled and said, "Come swimming."

"No. Oh no—in fact, I was really going to bed. You see, I didn't sleep."

The redhead looked at him. She was wearing a T-shirt over a bikini. On the T-shirt was the word *"SAMSARA."*

"I didn't either," she said. "I think it was the wine."

"The wine?"

"The hotel wine. It does strange things if you're not used to it."

"I had the wine too," Edward said suddenly and smiled.

"Then that's what it was."

"Yes. That's what it was. Of course. That's what it was."

"Come swimming then."

"Thank you but I'm not really—well, look at me."

Edward laughed nervously and then watched as Alice turned and walked down the steps. *It was the wine.*

From his balcony he tried to see her in the swimming pool but it was masked by a tree.

In his bed he slept in his dressing-gown and dreamt about Alice. It was an aesthetic dream. She was in white standing by a river. It appeared to be an English river, but in truth it could have been anywhere. He could see a willow tree and behind one of the branches there was a face staring at him. It wasn't Blanche and it wasn't Amy. It was a man, smoking a clay pipe. "Even in my dreams, even in my dreams," Edward called out, "you won't leave me alone." *If you love,* the *houngan* said, taking Edward's arm, *you will believe and you will see.* They were now walking along the parapet of a castle, the sea below them. *The more you show your love, the more the ghost will become clearer to you.* "You mustn't feed me this nonsense," Edward shouted, sitting by the fire, by the dogs. *Take away your friendship and the ghost will disappear.* "This nonsense," Edward repeated, running out of the rain towards the bridge, anglers turning, raising a finger to the mouth.

At eleven o'clock, Edward woke to find himself in the sunlit hotel room. Outside, there could be heard the sounds of other guests talking loudly by the pool, while in the distance martial music was being played on loudspeakers set around the football stadium. There was, as you will understand, comfort in this mundane reality. Edward, however, was no longer like us. He had, he thought, been through enough. He would leave Haiti and return to England before he began to question those absurd fantasies. That, he was sure, would be the end of it.

Reaching for a suitcase, he called out to Amy.

Entering her room, he looked at the bed. It was empty, remade as if it had never been slept in.

Amy herself was no longer there.

Part Four:
Late Sister Blanche

In the stumps of old trees where the rain gathers and the/trapped leaves and the beak, and the laced weasel's eyes, there are/holes the length of a man's arm, and at the bottom a sodden bible/written in the language of rooks. But do not put your hand down/to see, because

10

There was a note. As always there was a note, written in Amy's hurried scrawl, employing a green Pentel like a brush, circles replacing dots above the *i*'s. It was lying casually on a table, almost as if it were to be overlooked in order to be revealed later by the writer, saying, "Ah, there you see. I *told* you I had left a note." Edward found it after a few minutes, snatched it up, fearing the worst, and read the following:

> **Edward**
> *You were asleep. Didn't want to wake you. Gone to the beach. Ibo?*

That was all. No signature. Edward read it twice, then put it in his pocket and stood for a moment staring into space, unsure of what to do next. Through the partition door he could see his suitcase on the floor.

At the desk, dressed once more in blazer and flannels, he asked directions to the beach.

"Which one, monsieur?"

"Which one? I don't know. The nearest, I suppose."

"There are many," the clerk replied. In the lobby behind them someone was now playing the piano. The Creole in the Disney shirt. The tune, "Honeysuckle Rose."

"Well, where do people *usually* go?" Edward asked anxiously.

"That depends. Most people prefer the pool."

"I don't want the pool. I want the beach."

"Well, there is Kyona Beach—"

"Kyona?"

"Or of course there is Ibo Beach."

"Ibo? Yes. How do you spell that?"

"I–B–O. *Ibo.*"

"Yes. How far is that?"

"Thirty minutes perhaps. It is on Cacique Island."

"Could you write that down?"

"What?"

"What you said. The island. Cass—"

"Cacique. Any driver knows Ibo Beach, monsieur. The Saint-Marc road."

"If you could just write it down. Write it down here. On the back of this piece of paper. There."

In the taxi, Edward tried to convince himself that it wasn't Amy's fault. He had overslept, after all. She was just being kind. She had allowed him his sleep and left a message to say where she was. It was the natural thing to do. And yet he felt once again a sense of insecurity, of being manipulated. Before falling asleep, earlier, he had resolved that everything that happened while they remained in this wretched country would be *his* choice, *his* suggestion, because there was security in that. If there *was* a plot against him (and now it seemed so absurd analysed in sunlight, sitting in a Renault), it was he, Edward, who wanted to dictate the terms. In brief, pack his bags and go home. Bye-Bye.

"*C'est loin?*" Edward asked, leaning towards the driver. "*La plage?*"

"*Non.*"

"*Mais elle est sur une . . . une île? N'est-ce pas?*"

"Oui."

But, all things considered, it was only a question of going to a public beach. Water sports, shuffleboard, scuba, and snorkling. Such petty diversions as these.

"Elle est belle? La plage?"

Nothing could be sinister in that.

"Oui. Elle est belle."

Edward lowered the window and stared at the sea and the inevitable and endless rows of croton, some of the shrubs ten feet high, the ovate leaves green, yellow. Red. *"Oui, elle est belle,"* Edward repeated, then raised the window, despite the heat, and leant back sadly into a corner of the seat. He didn't look out of the window, nor say another word for the rest of the journey.

When Edward was a child he lived in a house that was popular with bats. A large house on a hill where a single bat would enter in the autumn if a window was left open, usually near the conservatory. The family had a routine in such emergencies, prefaced by the comforting phrase, "It won't ever touch you. Watch. It won't ever touch you if you shout." They looked forward to it, grownups holding towels as the creature darted back and forth, hiding under the stairs or behind a screen to reappear above them, retreating from the noise until it found the open door and disappeared. Not once did Edward see it touch anyone. Not even a little girl's hair.

The beach appeared to be designed for tourists. Set on a small island, it encouraged the wealthy to arrive in their yachts from Miami or Rio or even from the Mediterranean. Moored side by side, so the poor could stand in the deckle-edge of the sea and stare at the polished wood, the brass rails, a steward placing coloured napkins within wine-glasses. Music could be heard, the rich man's Muzak of quadraphonic rock and classical patter, and now and again a figure would appear from below deck, hands behind back to stare at the land or talk to a girl lying face down, breasts resting on cushions, reading a book she had begun at another harbour on another island. Some voyagers were even swimming in the water or walking on the land itself, but not many. Yachts, as we all know, you and I, are possessive toys. They rarely like to be left alone.

Edward didn't see Amy at first, and for a while he thought she wasn't on the beach at all. It had been a hoax to lure him away, something that she could laugh at as she stood on the balcony watching him being driven into the distance. One of her silly little games.

And then, of course, he saw her, lying on a beach-chair in the centre of the sand, eyes closed, leaning back, coins covering her eyes, wearing her white swimming costume. Her appearance took him by surprise, not the physical presence itself but the fact that he hadn't noticed her immediately. He felt as if he had walked past the spot where she lay at least twice, and even when he did see her she seemed to be in a haze, as if he were myopic and had forgotten his spectacles. There seemed to be no shape to her, nothing tangible until Edward realized that this mirage was due to the sun. It was behind her, reflecting on the white of the sand and consequently prone to distortion. On approaching the chair he could see her clearly, first the outline and then finally the features themselves, the skin rather pink and liable to burn. Beside her, another beach-chair, empty except for a towel draped over the back, the centre of the seat darker as if wet.

"Amy?"

There was no movement. It was possible she was asleep.

"Amy— Why didn't you wake me? You could have done that."

"I left a note."

The answer was said matter-of-factly, as if there was nothing more to explain, then the coins were removed from the eyes, one in each hand, and Amy looked up at Edward. She didn't smile.

"I left a note on the table."

"I know. I read it."

"Of course. That's why you're here. Dressed like that."

Edward stared at her. It wasn't his wife. It wasn't his Amy. He watched as she slowly raised her body, then turned over and settled herself down onto her stomach, one hand moving behind her to pull down the base of her costume over her thighs, fingers touching the skin under the nylon, lingering, then moving aside.

"Why don't you put on your trunks?" she asked, her voice muffled by her hair. "Those funny little bathing trunks you bought?"

"Amy?" Edward said, kneeling beside her. "Did you hear anything last night?"

"Last night? Should I have done?"

"Voices?"

Amy looked up, then poured some sun-tan oil onto the palm of her hand.

"Amy?" Edward repeated.

"But I sleep in a different room, Edward. How could I hear what you hear?" And then, "Oh dear, I hope I don't burn."

Edward stared at her. *It's one of her games,* he thought.

"Put some oil on my back, Edward. Where I can't reach."

He felt his hands on her spine, then lower at the base. The skin was hot, moist with the oil (a rivulet slid slowly across the waist, dropped to the chair) and Edward felt the muscles in Amy's body tense, the movement of her legs, then the muscles relaxed. She appeared to be asleep and from a distance he could see the details of her. It was then that his gaze was drawn to the sea.

The man was now the centre of attention. People on the yachts were moving to the rail, sunglasses were being placed over eyes; those on the rim of the tide stopped and turned, pretty girls leant forward, a frieze of faces, pouts, aahs, Pentax and Leica, waiters on terraces holding a tray in the air froze like caryatids, stomachs forward, as the man posed on the ninth wave aware of the admiration, visible to all; then the surfboard thrust forward, hovered in the air, ceased to move, before descending finally into the shallows, hesitating and coming to rest, a stationary pedestal for the silver surfer. There was no applause. As he stepped onto the sand the spectacle was over. That rare moment was complete. Around him, people ate, laughed, snoozed, waiters placed food into bowls, and the pretty girls allowed their bikinis to be removed in the coolness of cabins.

It was only Edward who stared at Azevedo as he walked up the beach towards him from the sea, the sun highlighting the dark skin, the broad shoulders. Azevedo waved, then began to run as he saw him, and as he approached he called out Edward's name enthusiastically, adding how pleased he was to see him again.

"I'll stay for lunch," Edward said to himself, glancing back towards Amy, still oblivious in her cocoon. "It would be selfish not to do that."

When Azevedo reached him he shook his hand and grinned. "I thought you might be here."

"But why?"

"Well, *everybody* comes here. Can't you see?"

Edward smiled shyly, then said, "I suppose you've seen Amy."

"Amy?" Azevedo asked, frowning, then looked across the beach. "Ah yes."

Silence. Then: "I'd better change. Don't you think?"

Edward glanced at him and noticed that Azevedo was not in fact wearing bathing trunks but white Jockey shorts. Edward stared at them, the water making them almost transparent, and looked away.

"It was either these or nothing at all," Azevedo said, smiling. "You see, I hadn't anticipated the beach either."

They decided not to disturb Amy immediately—she was now in her own limbo—and Edward waited while Azevedo changed into his clothes in one of the small cabanas that lined the beach. He could hear him showering, could see his feet under the wooden door, the left then the right disappearing, to be dried before finally both could be seen encased in their respective shoes, and Azevedo appeared, fully dressed, stepping into the light and saying, "Well, Edward, now I am ready." He was wearing the same clothes, the same beige suit and white silk shirt that he had worn since Edward and he had first met. It was possible that even the socks and shoes were the same.

"You don't mind me spending the day with you?" Azevedo said. "Please say if you do. It was just such a coincidence us meeting like this. . . ."

"No. Not at all. Of course not."

"It is possible that since you are on holiday you would like to be alone. Alone with your wife."

"No," Edward said quickly. "I'd like to be— I'd like you to be with us."

Azevedo glanced at him and smiled. "Thank you, Edward."

And so it was understood. They decided, the two men, to have lunch immediately, cocktails then lunch. Once again, Amy was not disturbed, not out of malice but simply because it was she who was now asleep, and it was she who was now left a note. In that respect, Edward had regained his role, as well as finding a replacement for his trust. The two men therefore walked side by side across the beach, an avenue of palms and bougainvillaea, towards a restaurant set on the shore facing the mainland. The Englishman, pink-faced, sandy hair, in blazer and flannels, striding, arms behind his back, head up, as if inspecting a guard of honour at Windsor or acknowledging a battalion of beaters at Balmoral. Beside him, the darker man, hands in pockets, the air of a successful man, an athlete, an actor, what you will. In the distance, to the left, a woman lying on a beach-chair is watching but does not move.

"You look tired, Edward."

They are sitting under a canopy of wisteria and vines. Edward and Azevedo. Between them, two whisky sours.

"I didn't sleep much last night."

"The heat perhaps."

"No. I think it was the wine."

"The wine? To me, the effect is usually the reverse. I sleep like a log."

"This time it was different."

Azevedo said nothing but by his attitude, immobile, watching Edward, he appeared to be waiting for Edward to continue. To explain. There was no demand, no overt request, and yet Edward felt obliged to elaborate—it would have been bad manners to do anything else.

"The holiday hasn't been what I expected. It hasn't been that."

"What *did* you expect?"

"You see, I never really wanted to come here. It wasn't my choice. It was Amy's."

"And now you regret it?"

Edward hesitated, glancing towards the beach. Amy was not in sight.

"When you look at us," he said, "when you see Amy and I together, what do you think?"

"In what sense?"

"Well, what do you think? Do you think we are happy together?"

"I hardly know you."

"But you observe. You know me much more than almost anyone else. What I said yesterday. . . ."

"You talked about yourself. But did you talk about Amy?"

"Didn't I? I must have done. Well, even if I didn't, doesn't that indicate something to you?"

"It indicates that you are no longer happy with her."

"Oh, God, do you think that?"

"No, Edward. You are telling me that."

"Then it is true. But you see, it is not like the usual story, husband and wife. One not understanding the other. That kind of thing. Our marriage is not like that. Never has been. I thought about it in the taxi coming here, trying to work out what exactly was wrong, and I believe I know some of the answers. Not all, but some. You see, when we married, in the first months, we established a relationship that we thought would go on forever. Unchanging. It was not an orthodox relationship but it was, I believe, how we wanted it. In a sense it was no different from before we even met. We just suddenly happened to be living, growing, side by side, in the same house, acknowledging each other's existence, and, I believe, grateful for that. We were happy, happier than anyone we knew. There were no quarrels, no bitterness. Just a friendship."

"Then you were lucky."

"I thought so. But it was a selfish existence. Selfish on my side at least. You see . . . we were never close. *Physically* close— Oh, dear, I shouldn't be saying this."

"Let us change the subject."

"I shouldn't be saying this because it amounts to a betrayal. But *I* am the one who is at fault. I had no desire for her. Do you understand what I mean?"

"I think so."

"Except in my mind. I would see her . . . I would see her when she was doing the most ordinary things. Reading a book. Standing in the garden considering a shrub—something silly like that. And I would desire her then. Sometimes so strongly that I could feel the touch of her. But if she suddenly came into the room, came into the room, into the bed, then . . . I would hate it if even a finger moved against mine. It would disgust me. It would make me shudder as if it were a spider that had crawled out of the bedcovers."

Edward looked away, his face red, and Azevedo lit a cigarette and placed the dead match neatly on the edge of the table.

"And how did Amy react to this?"

"She never complained. I believed then that she was contented that it should be that way. That she was like me. I suppose I convinced myself that. I never asked. I should have done, I know. But you must understand, if she had said otherwise, that she wanted . . . sex, the situation would still be the same. Except that I would know and I couldn't have lived with that. So I never asked. But, please believe me, it was a happy marriage. I never hurt her. I loved her and I still do."

"Then what made it change?"

"Change?"

"You said the marriage was no longer happy. That something happened."

Edward stared at Azevedo, assessing him, then was silent.

"You don't have to say anything, Edward."

"You couldn't guess what happened. No one could. You mustn't try."

"You said you loved someone else besides Amy."

"I said you mustn't try."

"The woman who died?"

"You mustn't try. It isn't what you think."

"I'm not thinking anything."

"What happened at Tewkesbury can never happen again. So you mustn't try to guess. It's finished. If only it was forgotten."

"That is why you came to Haiti?"

"Not Haiti exactly. To the Caribbean. It could have been anywhere. I wanted to see whether we could both be happy again. God knows I tried. I still do. I said to Amy that the fault was that we had never known each other. Never. Not once. I said that I wanted to try to find out about her. That she must give me that chance."

"And *are* you finding out about her?"

"Yes. And I wish I'd never tried. Do you mind me telling you all this?"

"No."

"You see, after we leave here, it is doubtful that you and I will ever see each other again. That would be sad. . . ."

"Yes. But you mustn't anticipate. . . ."

"But we must be realistic. We have different lives. And so I can talk to you. Unlike to a priest. One can only *confess* to them. I mean, as a form of monologue. A weekly bulletin. It eases the soul but it doesn't solve anything. I don't want a penance; I want an answer. Besides, how could I know that the priest I am talking to is not like the one who was at school with me." Edward suddenly smiled.

"Some poor wretch is entrusting his eternity to him at this very moment. Think of it." And then, "I think Amy is plotting against me."

Standing on the steps above the restaurant in a grove of bougainvillaea, they peered, one after the other, through a coin-operated telescope.

"She's still there. She hasn't moved," Edward said.

Walking back to the terrace, Azevedo asked, "Why did you say that about Amy . . . ?"

"Please forget I said that. It is that *houngan* who is corrupting her."

Azevedo suddenly stopped: "Which *houngan*?"

"Jean-Dantor."

"What did you say to him?"

"What?"

"What did you say to him?"

Edward stared at Azevedo, surprised by the tone of his voice.

"Nothing. Nothing at all. . . ."

"Edward, promise me you will not listen to anyone like Jean-Dantor. When I said I had enemies, I meant people like him."

"Oh, I assure you I wasn't taken in by what he said. You mustn't think that. I don't fall for nonsense like that. Not like Amy."

"It is not nonsense, Edward."

There was a silence. In the bay, to the south, someone in a yellow life-jacket was water-skiing.

"If only it was."

Dear Papa

Dear Papa dear Papa dear Papa. Dear Papa. Dear Papa Legba. Cher Papa Legba. Je t'aime. Tu es le Bon Dieu des Dieux. Je t'aime. Je t'adore. Je t'adore.

Sauve-moi,
Blanche

The clouds appeared abruptly, moving in from the east, blacking out the sun. Soon it would rain. Canopies were opened and shutters were closed and the sea was emptying of people. One or two yachts would raise anchor and leave.

"It'll only be a shower," Azevedo said. "A heavy shower but a shower nevertheless."

"We ought to go and find Amy."

"Yes."

The two men began to walk slowly back towards the cabanas along the beach.

"Do you think Jean-Dantor is evil?" Edward asked, not looking at Azevedo.

"He is a disciple of Baron Samedi. The God of Death."

"But you believe in what he said?"

"Forget about him."

"Forget about him?" Edward said, raising his voice. "How can you expect me to do that *now*?"

Azevedo didn't answer. Stunned, Edward suddenly ran in front of him, stopping him: "Don't tell me you also believe in ghosts? That talk about ghosts?"

He stared at Azevedo, who hesitated, then stepped aside and walked on.

"You of all people," Edward said.

Amy was now walking beside them. She had changed back into her dress and was carrying her swimming costume and a towel in a transparent plastic bag. On the front, a picture of Mickey Mouse.

"Now what are you two talking about?" she asked.

Neither man answered.

11

The rain came down in force as they reached the mainland.
"We ought to find some shelter," Edward called out as they ran along the quay. "All the taxis have gone."

"But where?"

The water was now soaking the three of them, Amy's hair layered to her face, her white dress darkening against her breasts and legs.

"I don't know. Anywhere."

To the right, fifty yards away, a row of shanty houses, fringing the waterfront. They were known as *cailles,* and were nothing more than handmade wooden walls (sometimes covered by plaster, sometimes by straw, often neither), surrounding a carpet of earth. Inside, an intruder might find mats covering the floor made of the branches of a banana tree, though these were not to walk on but to sleep on. Little else, except of course the icons. In the higher parts of Haiti, away from the docks, in the *coumbite,* the *cailles* may well be painted, more colourful, and pictures may cover a wall celebrating one fantasy or another. But here, there was no attempt at decoration. They were simply amenities, whatever that may imply.

"In there," Edward said, pointing to the nearest shack. A painted sign, faded, reading "Yankee Bar." It was a euphemism. Beneath it, a collage of graffiti that now seemed as apposite as *Cave Canem* at Pompeii.

"Are you sure it's appropriate?" Azevedo replied and smiled.

"Well, at least we can wait there till the rain stops."

"Please. I'm soaked," Amy shouted, removing her shoes.

Azevedo smiled again and they entered the beaded doorway, stepping over rotting mangoes, tins, sundry matters.

Inside, it was indeed drier, though water still filtered through the cracks in the tin roof, or beat on the tin itself, an incessant timpany. At first it seemed, in the half-light, as if the shack was empty. A makeshift bar could be seen, one or two bottles, a table. On the walls, a series of primitive images and designs, the latter resembling enlargements of snowflakes, the former more human, benign faces of men and more often of a woman. There was also a statue of this same woman, pious in pose like a Virgin Mary, except that the figure was naked. Beside it, a candle.

"Who is that?" Amy asked as she reached for a towel from her bag.

"The woman," Azevedo replied, "is Grande Erzulie."

"Who?"

"Grande Erzulie is a goddess. *The* goddess. Men worship her, pray to her. Fall in love with her."

"She doesn't look like a goddess."

"That is her face there as well. And there. She is the goddess of many things."

Amy glanced at Azevedo, then at the statue, and moved closer to it. Almost as if in ritual she reached up and touched the mahogany of the legs and then placed her fingers on the roundness of the stomach, index finger resting in the pleat.

"What things?" she asked.

"Fertility," Azevedo replied.

There was a silence, and then Amy suddenly laughed. She did not move her hand.

"And that painting," Azevedo said, as if nothing had happened,

Nightshade 126

"represents God the Father, if you wish. Le Bon Dieu des Dieux. He is called Papa Legba."

It was then that Amy began to shiver.

"You'll catch cold," Edward said. "Amy, you know how easily you become ill."

He was nervous. The icons, the noise of the rain, small creatures scuttling into dark corners.

"I'll be all right," Amy answered.

"But look at you. That thin dress."

"I have no other."

"Perhaps if you dried yourself. There must be another room where you can dry yourself. You can put on your bathing costume again. That must be dry. Wear it under your dress."

"Oh, don't be silly, Edward."

Edward blushed, a sudden anger.

"I just don't want you to be ill, that's all."

Azevedo watched all this as if he were a mere passer-by who had stopped to observe a minor incident before walking on.

"A drink might help," he said casually. "It will warm you up."

Edward nodded, peering round the room. "But why is there no one here?" he said.

Azevedo shrugged. No idea.

"Well surely we ought not to be in here," Edward continued, anxiously. "I mean it could be private or—"

He then stopped, quite suddenly, his mouth open, and stared across the dirt floor towards the rear of the bar, towards a door. A boy had appeared, black, and was standing watching him. It is possible that he had been there for some time. The boy was also naked, unconsciously so, as if he had never worn clothes in his life, which, by his appearance, the slight erection, the suggestion of pubic hair, was about twelve years all told.

"Pleasss?" the boy hissed, grinning. "Pleasss?"

Edward immediately looked away, retreating towards the outer door, stumbling, and glanced despairingly at Amy; but she hadn't moved. Instead, she was staring at the boy, from head to toe, with the same expression of curiosity as she had observed the statue. One was conscious of the humidity.

"*Coque-tel?*"

No one answered and Edward found himself turning, despite himself, and glancing back towards the bar. The boy was looking at him, his gaze steady, as if there was no one else in the room. As if he had been selected.

"N-n-n . . ." Edward stammered.

"*Rhum. m'sieur? Pleasss?*"

"No—we must—*on fait*—"

"*Pa pi mal, m'sieur, Merci*"

The boy then began to walk towards Edward holding out his hand. Oh God, don't they know I can't swim?

"*Pa pi mal.*"

"Just give him a coin," Azevedo said quietly from the shadows. "Then he will leave."

"But why? I can't—*Amy*?"

"Just give him a coin."

"*Pa pi mal, m' sieur.*"

Fumbling, Edward dropped a coin in the boy's hand, not looking at him, and the boy then walked to the bar, reached up, and seemed to pose, his naked back towards Edward, the small bottom thrust out, then took down a bottle of Rhum Barbancourt and placed it on the table.

"*Moi?*" the boy then asked, eyes wide, re-turning his gaze towards Edward. Why me? Why is he only talking to me?

"*T' vois moi?*"

Near the statue, Amy watched, lower lip under upper teeth, hair smeared to her face, watching each movement of the nakedness, watching as the boy's erection began to swell, rising, as if demonstrating that his merchandise had at least some form of guarantee. She then heard Edward shout out loud, and then he was gone, clawing at the beaded curtain and disappearing into the daylight.

There was a silence as Azevedo slowly walked to the door and stared towards the jetty.

"I think the rain has stopped," he said finally and looked at Amy and smiled.

They found Edward at the beginning of the landing stage, pressed against the wall of a warehouse.

"Why didn't you tell me that place was—"

"A brothel," Azevedo said quietly.

"That place was . . . *that*?"

"But *you* chose it, Edward."

Edward looked at him, then at Amy. She was standing in profile, hair combed back neatly.

"I think we ought to go back to the hotel," he said.

"Then I'll leave you here."

It was Azevedo who had spoken. Amy turned towards him, was about to say something, then was silent.

"But I'll walk you to a taxi."

The streets surprisingly were empty (rain, siesta), except for one or two drunks who stared at them from doorways, and some old men who were playing *zo,* a local game of dice.

"Is this La Saline?" Amy asked.

"No," Azevedo replied. "La Saline is worse. How did you know about La Saline?"

"I was told about it. Someone I knew had been there."

"I hope it wasn't at night."

"I don't know."

They had now reached a small cobbled square. On one side there stood a large colonial house, tall columns and windows the height of each room. Discreet carvings above a door. It was now empty, in ruins, boarded up, and had been since the Revolution of 1804. A ballroom was used to store sisal.

Later, they saw a taxi parked near the edge of the Iron Market.

"Perhaps we could see each other tonight?" Azevedo asked.

Amy didn't reply, looking away. Azevedo glanced at Edward.

"Yes," Edward said. "Yes, of course."

Amy looked at both men, folded her arms, turning her back on them, then said abstractedly, "You see, Edward. There are no beggars here either."

"Too poor to beg," Azevedo replied.

Edward stared at him and said, "That's what Amy said."

A pause, then: "It's a popular proverb," Azevedo answered. "Like 'Stupidity doesn't kill you but it sure makes you sweat.' One hears them all the time."

In the taxi back to the Dessalines, Edward thought about the boy in the Yankee Bar. "I don't understand why he only talked to *me*," he said out loud. "As if I was the only one there."

"Who?"

"That black . . ."

Passing the Presidential Palace, Edward murmured, "It was a coincidence that Dan—that Azevedo was at the beach. Wasn't it, Amy?"

"What?"

"Of all places."

"He hardly said a word to me."

"You were sleeping, Amy."

"Don't forget it was *you* who agreed to meet him again tonight."

Entering the driveway of the hotel, Edward said, "Who would have thought he believed in voodoo?"

"It was *your* idea about tonight, Edward. Remember that."

"An educated man like that."

In the late afternoon, Edward took tea alone on the hotel terrace. Amy had said that she wanted to rest, that the sun had possibly burnt her skin and that she wanted to stay in the coolness of her room. Edward didn't mind. He found himself thinking of Azevedo, of the image of him appearing from the sea. *Is it unnatural that I should think of him like this?* he thought. And, in a sense, one must suppose that it was.

"Hello."

A pair of sun-tanned legs and the lower half of a bikini, set low on the hips, were now dominating his eyeline. Edward looked up and saw Alice.

"Where have you been all day?"

Edward stared at her. She was standing very close and he could smell Ambre Solaire and the odour of musk. Of her body. He suddenly wanted to reach out and touch her skin, feel its warmth.

"I went to the beach," Edward said quickly and concentrated on drinking his tea.

"God, did you? Aren't they awful?"

"What?"

"The beaches here. Are they still full of tourists?"

"Well, we're tourists too, aren't we?" Edward glanced up and added, "At least *I* am."

Alice pulled a face, then grinned, a constellation of freckles now visible on each side of her nose.

"How are you feeling now?" she asked, leaning against a pillar and looking down at him. "You look much better than this morning."

"Why, thank you."

"You look really— Well, a hundred times better."

"Thank you."

Edward was now beginning to blush but, oddly, for the first time, he didn't mind. He was flattered by the attention.

"How was the swimming?" he asked.

"Oh, fine," Alice said. "Except for the chlorine. They always put too much chlorine in the pool. It used to be all right once."

Edward nodded. "Do you want some tea?"

"No thank you. I'm going to the cinema."

"The cinema?"

"Yes. Haven't you ever been to it? It's open-air. They show American films mostly. Pretty dreadful." She laughed and added, "Westerns and things like that. Sometimes, though, there's a good film."

"Where is it?"

"Over there." Alice pointed across the gardens to the west. "If you keep walking in that direction you'll see it."

"Oh."

"I saw *Brief Encounter* last week. Imagine? In the middle of Haiti, *Brief Encounter*. I always cry in that. Don't you?"

"Well, no."

"You don't?"

"I mean I haven't seen it. Is it sad?"

"The saddest."

Alice sighed and sat down opposite Edward, selecting a biscuit from a plate but not eating it. Suddenly, Edward felt self-conscious, almost guilty, sitting at a table talking to a girl like this. He glanced around, fearing to see Amy, but she wasn't there. Only Lapôtre standing by the bar.

"Good-bye," Alice said suddenly, standing up.

"What?"

Alice looked at him. "I ought to change. I can't go to the cinema like this."

"Are you sure you wouldn't want some tea? It's not very good but—"

" 'Bye."

The redhead began to walk away.

"Wait a minute," Edward called after her. He was like a child.

Alice stopped and smiled.

"Are you going there alone?"

"Good-bye," she said.

Edward watched her walk away, studying her back, the shape of her bottom.

In his room, Edward peered through the half-open partition door, holding his breath.

"Amy?" he whispered again and was relieved to see that she was asleep.

Standing before the mirror, Edward combed his hair. He was suddenly aware that the hair was thinning above the temples. He had never noticed that before, never been conscious of this vanity. The blazer too was no longer as smart, as stylish as he had believed. Tomorrow, he resolved, he would buy a new suit. A beige one, perhaps, like the one worn by Azevedo. He deserved that luxury.

Later, walking across the gardens, the hotel now no longer in sight, he heard the music. It seemed distorted, as if it were raining and he could hear voices. A man and a woman.

"*Good night. Kathy. See you tomorrow.*"

Lights flickered in the leaves of palms, a reflection from a wall that was now before Edward, towering above him.

"*Good night, Don. Take care of that throat. You're a big singing star now—remember? This California dew is a little heavier than usual tonight.*"

He could now see the faces, black, all gazing upwards in the same direction. Some of the audience sat on the grass, some on benches. He could also see the screen, see his shadow.

"*Really? From where I stand, the sun is shining all over the place.*"

Then, as he walked quickly on the sidelines, stepping over small children, he saw Alice. She was sitting alone, a solitary girl with red hair and a white T-shirt, index finger between her teeth. On the screen, a man was dancing in pouring rain, holding a rolled-up umbrella. Beside Alice, the bench was empty. Edward hesitated, then slowly walked towards her until he was standing close enough to touch her. But she didn't look around, nor make any indication that she was aware of his presence. Her attention was solely on the screen before her, a rectangle of rain and music against the backdrop of the clear Haitian sky, the colour of saffron. It is possible that Edward stood unnoticed for five minutes, and by then he knew it was too late. The moment had gone and the self-conscious guilt returned. Frightened to make a sound he walked away, back towards the hotel. Once he stopped and glanced back, but Alice was in darkness, hidden by trees.

"It would have been foolish of me to have stayed," he said, "a married man of my age."

The departure, however, was regretted.

At seven o'clock, this same evening, Edward sat in his socks in his room in the Valentino Suite, sipping at a whisky. He had ordered a bottle and it had been delivered accompanied by two monogrammed glasses, two green swizzle-sticks with naked ladies on the top, a plastic bucket of ice, four paper napkins, two paper coasters, a jug of water, a long-handled spoon, a dish of olives, half a dozen toothpicks, and a bill. Half an hour later, Edward had drunk a quarter of the bottle and was feeling relaxed and not a little drunk. It was a preparation for the arrival of Azevedo.

"He didn't say when he would be here? Didn't say, did he, Amy?" he called out towards the closed partition door. It was a shout to frighten the bats.

Amy herself had not been seen since that furtive glance after tea. Nor had he heard her cough or move around.

"I suppose it's dinner. Would be, wouldn't it?"

There was no reply. It appeared, as Edward said out loud, to be a habit lately.

Pushing open the partition door he thought immediately that he was more drunk than he had anticipated, for the room seemed to be moving. However, it was only the heavy metal lamp in the centre of the ceiling that was swaying back and forth. The cause, as Edward could now see, was due to the fact that something was hanging from it, obliterating the shade and leaving only a circle of light on the wall, floor, wall below. The shutters were closed. Oh dear, Edward thought, she's hanged herself.

"Amy!" he screamed, stumbling over a chair, grasping towards the lamp. And then he was running along the corridor into sunlight, onto grass, neatly cut north to south. He could see ducks on the lawn (mallards, Muscovies, pretty little things), the croquet mallets, an abandoned sweater.

"It's Blanche," he called out, but Amy didn't appear to hear. She was sitting smiling at him, holding up a Sunday newspaper and pointing to a picture, a drawing of a pair of shoes. "Blanche!" Edward repeated and ran back towards the house. To his left, he could see guests arriving, children sitting in the back of a Cortina, someone waving through the windscreen.

In the bedroom, Blanche was still there. Drawing back the curtains, it was noticed that she was wearing a long white dress decorated in neat bows and lace and white silk buttons on the sleeves. Edward didn't recognize it at first, until it was pointed out that it was Amy's wedding dress. There was a veil but that couldn't be found.

"Amy!" Edward called out again, retreating towards the door.

"Yes?" Amy said.

She was sitting before the dressing-table, her back to him, peering into the mirror. On her shoulders and nose was Pond's Cold Cream. The room was now filled with light as the lace coverlet fell from the lamp into Edward's arms.

"It's too bright," Amy said. "Put it back."

Edward stared at the coverlet on the floor. It was white in colour and rather delicate, with a frond of silk around the border. Treading on it, he said, "You did that deliberately, Amy."

"What?"

"That."

"What?"

Amy turned and looked at the floor and the lamp.

"I never thought," she said. "Believe me, I never thought. I'm sorry."

These words may be true. It would be unfair to misjudge her for the mere shading of a lamp.

"You ought to get ready, Amy," Edward said, leaving the room, returning to his chair.

We are now on the eighth day.

12 In his own room, Edward drank a further three glasses of whisky and did not realize he was drunk until he tried to write in his diary. He found that he could not employ the pen properly, and that what he wanted to write (holiday doggerel, perhaps) appeared gibberish and confused. One sentence seemed to read "Fia Fur Bis Fle" and there seemed no motive to it. Something he had read once, he assumed, in a Latin grammar.

Washing his face in cold water, breathing in night air, he returned to Amy's room. She was still sitting before the dressing-table (the lace coverlet folded and placed in a drawer out of sight), but was now wearing a green dress. Edward stared at her, stared at her reflection in the mirror, and then said, "What have you done to your face?"

"What?"

"What have you done to your face?"

"Why are you shouting?"

"I'm not shouting."

"You've been drinking."

"I have not been—"

Edward stopped before the venial sin, and said quietly, "Amy, you've done something to your face. I can see it from here."

"It's just eye-shadow."

"Eye-shadow? You've never licked—never *liked* things like that before."

Silence.

"*Amy?*"

"I thought it would make a change."

Edward walked nearer and stared at her both in the mirror, then directly, standing back, arms folded, before shaking his head as if auditioning a soubrette.

"No. Sorry."

"What do you mean—'Sorry'?"

"It doesn't suit you."

"It's just an experiment."

"But does it have to be green?"

"It matches the dress."

"I never liked that dress either."

"*I* do."

Amy then stood up and stared at Edward, almost in a pose of defiance.

"Look at *you,*" she said. "You've never had your hair combed like that before."

"Combed like *what?*" Edward shouted, and then heard Amy say, turning away, "Can we convince ourselves that we are doing all this for each other?"

There was a silence, broken only by Amy answering her own question, almost with sadness. No.

In the corridor, they walked in silence, politely, Edward leading the way. At one point, reaching a window overlooking a paved atrium outside, decorated with mulberry and vine, Edward saw Alice. She had her back to his, was leaning over a table, and appeared to be drawing on a piece of paper—but she may well have been simply writing a letter. To whom? Edward thought. A man? He assumed, in a way, that it had to be. Fortunate creature.

The Lyttons decided tacitly that they would wait in the lobby. No definite arrangements had been made, and so it was assumed that Azevedo would meet them at their hotel.

"If there are any calls for Lytton," Edward said to the desk-clerk, "we are in the lobby. Over there."

But after half an hour they were still there, still sitting in the same chairs, and still glancing constantly between the main door and the desk. People entered and left, guests greeted visitors who always seemed to arrive before one's own, and brief greetings were exchanged, but no more. The olives and the salted nuts were eaten, but Azevedo didn't arrive. Three times, Edward went to the desk, only to return to his arm-chair, shake his head, and stare fixedly at the wall. Naturally, he spoke, but they were mere platitudes, rhetorical statements, such as: "It's not the same as England. Everything happens much later abroad;" or "If he said he would be here, he'll be here." But as the minutes passed, Edward became less convinced. He grew restless, anxious, irritated by the pianist, by the laughter from others, and by Lapôtre, who had been watching them from his chosen bamboo chair by the door, cane across his knees.

But the main source of irritation was Amy herself. Throughout all this, the waiting, Edward's impatience, she had not moved but simply sat, arms folded, chin raised, facing her audience in the lobby. For that really is the impression she gave; and if no one had ever noticed Amy Lytton before, even in the most casual way, they were aware of her now. And that was the tragedy of it. Other women (Alice for example, or that dear lady from Michigan) exhibited less above the neck and more below, but it was the pathetic vulgarity of her appearance that was so obvious, and, in this respect, Edward was right. Her nails had been painted red, a pair of silver shoes had been found, lipstick had overlapped the edges of her mouth. She was, in truth, a sad creature to behold and there is no other word for it. But then, who are *we* to blame her? She had never learnt any better.

And yet, paradoxically, in the way she sat, the way she posed, it was as if Amy had suddenly realized the person she was, had banished all her innermost inhibitions to the closet where they belonged, and had said to the world, *"There* you are. *This* is how I am." She had discovered a confidence, and in that confidence (misguided as it was) she had sensed admiration, or, rather, attention, and was not disappointed. Quite the reverse. Amy enjoyed it, wanted it, and let us not deny her that. I myself cannot define it, but then there is no need. We all understand.

As for Edward, poor fool, it could only produce confusion. Suddenly, within minutes, while he had sat in his socks staring at the ceiling, there had been a transformation. The woman he had pitapatted with for four years, who had listened to his trite stories, had accompanied him from one dire ruin to another, had spurned his Chesterton and his Jemima Puddleduck (Ah, *that* must have hit below the belt), was now an apparent stranger to him. Someone he couldn't understand. He knew it wasn't just the green paint or the green dress, though he criticized them, for they, at least, were tangible. He knew it was something more, and there was his bewilderment.

"I don't know what all these people are staring at," he said. And then, "Well, he obviously isn't going to turn up."

"What?"

"I said he's obviously not going to turn up. You've got dressed up like—like *that* for nothing. You'll have to scrape it all off."

There was no reaction. Amy merely narrowed her eyes so that the daubs of green were more visible.

"It's quite obvious that he must have other friends," Edward continued. "*Women* friends. A man like him. His looks . . ."

Amy smiled and said, "You ought to know, Edward. You obviously know him better than I do."

"What do you mean by that?"

"Tête-à-tête."

"Tête-à-tête?"

"Tête-à-tête."

"Oh, don't be absurd."

"You're blushing, Edward."

"I'm not—"

"Tête-à-tête."

Out of the corner of his eye, Edward could see Lapôtre. See him smile and lift his hand. Nearby, the pianist turned over a page of music, considered the opening bars, then closed the book and decided to improvise. An early ballad by Rodgers and Hart that had lately become popular again in one place or another.

"Don't make me say things I'll regret, Amy," Edward said calmly. *Discipline of the Mind.* "Or do things that will hurt you." *Discipline of the Body.* No doubt, the poor soul was entertaining thoughts of Alice.

Amy stared at Edward, her face pale, recognizing this pathetic trait in his character. If only, she wished, he would hit me. Just once. She deserved that at least. To feel his hand on her body, no matter what the intention. God knows, she had provoked him enough.

She watched as Edward stood up, adjusted the flaps of his jacket, said "I'll try and telephone him. I should have thought of that before," and walked steadily across the lobby towards the desk without looking back. *Mercifully,* Amy thought, *I have my dreams.*

The desk-clerk handed the telephone book to Edward, and he opened it to find *Azevedo, D.* in the middle of the tenth page. Writing down the number he repeated it to the operator, and waited anxiously near the bar, the telephone at his ear, as she dialled. There was no reply. Only a single monotone.

"Il est mort," the operator said.

"What did you say?"

"The line is dead."

"Dead? Do you mean, out of order?"

"Perhaps."

Replacing the receiver, Edward was about to move away when Lapôtre approached him, gazing up at him: "Monsieur Lytton, can I be of help?"

"No. We are supposed to be meeting someone and . . ."

"So I thought. And they are late."

"They?"

"The people you are meeting. Do I know them?"

Edward hesitated, then shook his head and hurried on.

"No one keeps time in Haiti, Monsieur Lytton. Life here lasts forever."

"Yes. . . ."

Lapôtre was walking beside him, touching his arm.

"It is tragic about those Americans, don't you think? And you saw the accident as well."

Edward studied the black features of the Negro—the bald head, gold teeth. Behind him, on the wall, he could see the portrait of Phoebe Stanley.

"Excuse me," he began. "I must . . ."

"Of course. *Ça va sans dire. Ça va seins durs,*" Lapôtre replied smiling. "But please have a drink with my compliments. Anything."

The Negro bowed, clicked his heels, and walked away, snapped his fingers at the barman, then left the lobby altogether. In a private office, a telephone call was put through. And answered.

In the lobby, a man in a butterfly tie (McNab, an illusionist, frequenter of motels, hotels) was talking to Amy, leaning towards her and smiling Flattery. On his cuffs, *Playboy* cuff-links. As Edward approached, the man glanced at him, blinked, hesitated, then backed away, his hands signalling innocence.

"Who was that old man?" Edward asked, glaring at his wife.

"A man," Amy replied calmly.

"Do you know him?"

"No."

"*No?* Then what did he want? Standing there?"

Amy raised her shoulders imperceptibly, gazed into space for a moment, then glanced at Edward.

"Was there any answer on the telephone?"

"He was trying to pick you up, wasn't he? Dressed like that."

"Perhaps."

"*I* don't think it's funny."

"He said he liked my dress."

Amy began to smile, then looked away, hand over her mouth.

There was a pause, and then Edward said, "I'm going to wait outside."

"Not because of that man . . ."

"No. I think it best if I wait outside. It's obvious that Az— that he wouldn't meet us in the lobby. In public."

He glanced back towards Lapôtre, who was standing by the desk now, talking to one of the taxi-drivers.

"Why do you say that?" Amy asked.

"Because . . ."

Two drinks were placed before them, mint juleps, and Edward stared at them, ignoring them. The hideous swizzle-sticks.

"He has enemies," Edward said quietly.

Outside, in the darkness, husband and wife sat on opposite ends of a bench watching the driveway and the road, and then just staring into space at the silhouettes of trees.

"Edward," Amy said finally, her voice hesitant. "We're not friends any more, are we? Not like we were."

"Perhaps something has happened to him," Edward said.

"Do you think I've changed?"

"But then it wasn't a definite appointment. Nothing was planned."

"Do you, Edward? Think I've changed?"

Her voice was not one of concern exactly but more curiosity, like someone asking an opinion about a new hairstyle or the wearing of a small brooch.

"Yes," Edward replied casually.

"Do you mean the dress?"

"What? No. More than that."

He was not interested. He was watching the lights of an approaching taxi.

"How do you mean, 'More than that'?"

"I just liked you as you were."

The taxi reached the bench, illuminating the two people, wife leaning towards husband, husband staring anxiously at the passing car, and then the taxi had passed by. In the back seat, a man and a woman, the man smoking a panatela.

"As I was?" Amy asked.

"Yes."

The taxi stopped, a flicker of brake-lights. A porter could be seen hurrying down the steps, opening the trunk, and removing luggage.

"Do you mean last year? Last month? When?"

Amy's voice had suddenly become more incisive, surprising Edward, and he turned towards her.

"Last week, Edward? As I was last week? *How* was I last week?"

"Amy—"

"You must tell me. I want to know."

Her face was close to him, leaning across the bench. He could smell perfume, could see the green paint flaking, could smell sweat.

"Look," he said, retreating into the corner of the seat, "Let's not start an argument."

"But we never argue."

The new arrivals were now walking up the steps behind the porter, stopping to admire the architecture, like every tourist before them.

"Amy—all I said was—"

"I want to know, Edward. You said you liked me as I was."

"I didn't mean it like that."

"But that's what you said—"

"I know. I just— Oh, this is absurd. I just don't understand you lately."

"Tell me."

Nearby, a group of black children had stopped and were watching them, grinning.

"Not here," Edward said, lowering his voice. "Let's not quirrel— let's not *quarrel* here."

"Where then?"

"I don't want to quarrel anywhere."

"In your room?"

"No—"

"In *my* room?"

"Amy—"

"In my bed? Can we not quarrel there? Please?"

Amy was staring at him, a sudden trembling.

"Please. . . ."

143 Late Sister Blanche

Her mouth was slightly open, and he could hear her breathing, irregular, small gasps like a child who stage-manages tears.

"Before it's too late, Edward."

He seemed to see the very pores in her skin, the microscopic details of hair and lines; the purple aberration of a spot discovered on her neck. The new moon of dirt under a finger-nail. And then suddenly she was laughing, laughing not *with* him, not anything like that. But at him. And then she was gone. She was no longer there.

She had got up and was hurrying back towards the hotel, stumbling, then reaching the steps without looking back. It had happened so quickly that Edward hadn't even moved, and even now he didn't, but remained, his face reddening, ignoring the overt curiosity of the children. He should have followed Amy, he knew that; but the poor fool stubbornly remained, sitting there for a further half hour gazing at the road long after he realized that Azevedo would not appear that evening. Or perhaps ever again. "Before it's too late, Edward." Now what kind of nonsense is that?

Finally, as one or two lights in the hotel began to go out, Edward returned reluctantly to the lobby. At the desk, he asked if there were any messages—even though he knew there wouldn't be. The clerk made no reaction, but simply stared at Edward not saying a word.

"I asked whether there were any messages? My name is Lytton."

The clerk now seemed to be unsure what to do, glancing around him.

"Is anything the matter?" Edward asked, and then felt something damp touch his hand. Small black-and-pink fingers. Looking down he saw Lapôtre.

"Monsieur Lytton— It is your wife."

"Amy? What's happened? Where is she?"

"It's all right. She was just a little upset."

"What do you mean—'Upset'?"

The pianist was now studying the painting of Phoebe Stanley.

"A little hysterical."

Edward began to run across the lobby.

"The maid heard her screaming."

"Screaming?"

There was a sudden feeling of panic. It couldn't be true. They were talking of someone else. This little black bastard was all part of the same plot.

"Good *heavens*! Hello! And are you with the Tompkins lot as well?"

Who is this man? What is he gibbering about?

"The same package tour? And how are you enjoying it?"

"Enjoying it?"

"We've just arrived. We met at the last place, remember?"

It was as if he was in someone else's dream. *I am in someone else's dream.* He found himself stopping, shaking hands, being offered a panatela, being asked how the food was.

"My name's Parkins."

"Yes, I remember."

"From Burnstow."

"Yes, I remember."

"We met at that barbecue on the beach."

"Of course."

"And how is the weather here? And have you seen Baby Doc? And how long are you staying here? And is everything as filthy filthy as they say?"

Edward began to speak, shout, and then he was following Lapôtre, hurrying past closed doors until he could see his room, could see two strangers, a maid and a man with a valise, standing looking into the open door. Reaching it he saw Amy. She was pressed against a wall near the window, hiding her face.

Someone said, "The doctor wanted to give her a sedative, but she refused."

Somebody else said, "She seems better now."

"Leave us alone a moment," Edward asked, and entered the room, closing the door. He didn't speak immediately but looked around him. Nothing seemed to be disturbed. There was no chaos. Everything was neat and tidy, spick and span.

"Amy?"

Approaching her he saw her flinch, and then, like a child, she tried to hide her face away from him.

"Amy? What happened?"

There was no answer. Edward touched her, brought her a glass of water, touched her shoulder, the green dress, then sat down. He would wait. It had happened before, incidents like this. Not often, but enough to know how to cope. He picked up a magazine and began to look at the advertisements (a rather amusing one for Guinness), and then discovered an article on Victorian country houses. In one of the pictures he recognized Bestwood Lodge, in Nottinghamshire, designed by Teulon. It was an intriguing photograph, of the porch and oriel, taken in 1867, in which family and guests had chosen to be included, standing on the steps and leaning out of the window. A bearded man in profile wore a top hat and a woman carried an open parasol. Behind them, others, but they were in the shadows and only their hands could be seen and the tip of a nose.

"I heard Blanche singing," Amy said. "In the room above. I heard her singing as she used to sing when she was taking a bath."

13 The room was empty and had been since the occasion of the man on the balcony, as Edward knew. The previous guest, Mr. James, had left on that day, and the suite was not due to be occupied until the following morning. Nevertheless, Edward, Amy, and the maid walked up the first flight and into the corridor towards the suite. Nothing was said by Edward regarding the details of the incident, not only because he felt such matters were private but also because of something more profound. To be honest, Edward didn't believe a word of Amy's story, though he never said as much. This may, at first, seem somewhat startling; but if one considers it more carefully, then a justification for Edward's reaction can be found. To believe Amy, Edward considered, was to believe in ghosts and that, of course, was farcical. Blanche was dead. He had cut her down and they had buried her and that was the end of it.

True, he too had experienced bizarre occurrences that only Blanche (or someone who knew her) could have administered, but he still believed there was a logical, albeit disturbing, explanation. Someone was playing a sinister game and what better way of allaying suspicion if that "someone" pretended to be prey to the same visitations. *The*

Discipline of the Mind. And yet could Edward seriously consider such thoughts about Amy? His own wife?

Reaching the first floor, pushing open the door of the room (The Zeugma) Edward glanced at Amy. Her face was expressionless, pale, a slight trembling, and at that moment she looked very vulnerable, so that he wanted to reach over and take her hand and comfort her. Such was the paradox.

The maid led the way, and they could see immediately that the room was unoccupied, drawers and cupboards were empty, menu, stationery, and hotel guide placed neatly on a table awaiting new arrivals.

"I told you there was no one in here," Edward said.

In the bathroom, they found a dress on the floor tangled with underclothes and a pair of blue shoes as if removed before entering the bath. According to Amy, it was the kind of dress that Blanche would wear. It was her colour, her design. There was nothing else in the room. Nothing was disturbed. The bath was dry.

For the rest of that evening, Amy hardly said a word. She gave the impression that she was in a state of shock, and this may well have been true. Tranquilizers were prescribed; but it is unclear whether they were taken, since Amy locked herself in her room and refused to discuss the matter with anyone; and, in truth, Edward hardly tried.

"We are leaving Haiti as soon as possible," was all he said. It was the only positive action he could consider.

Amy never replied, indicating in her eyes neither assent nor refusal; and then, before closing her door, asked, "Did Azevedo arrive? Did you see him?"

It seemed to Edward an unexpected question and he hesitated, and then shook his head. For a brief moment he thought he saw Amy smile, not maliciously but reminiscent of those smiles adopted by Day Nurses and healthy Scottish nannies when directed towards their charge. It is a clumsy image, to be sure, but it is Edward's, and so one is stuck with it.

When the partition door was closed, Edward suddenly experienced an overwhelming feeling of depression. He began to shiver, his hands began to shake, and he could hear his breathing. He considered the whisky and, reaching for it, his gaze rested on the dress and the underclothes that he had pushed behind a chair, as if to banish them from his memory. His fingers touched the zip, the cotton, the coldness of the inside of a left shoe. He held the dress in his hand (the label was English, a silk lozenge embroidered with the name of the designer), and he could smell the odour of a perfume as well as of decay—familiar, distinctive, but regrettably unidentifiable. "I don't associate it with Amy," he said, then returned the garments to the floor. After ten minutes, he went to the door and hurried along the corridor towards the lobby.

The desk-clerk (the night replacement, a white American in a toupee from Baton Rouge) was pleasant but unhelpful.

"How long ago did you say she stayed here, sir?"

"Well, I'm not *certain* it was this hotel, but it must have been at least five years ago. Six perhaps."

"Oh. Then her name wouldn't be in this register, sir."

"I realize that. But there must be records, mustn't there?"

"I don't know. I assume so. You see, I'm only here temporarily, sir. Usually I cover the Primaries. Like Teddy White."

"Couldn't you find the records for me?" Edward asked impatiently.

"What? Oh, not now, sir. They'd be locked in the office. But if you ask tomorrow, the manager I'm *sure* would—"

"But couldn't you ask him tonight?"

"I could, but he's not here."

"Where is he? What about the assistant manager? *Is* there an assistant manager?"

But the clerk had moved away and was answering a telephone, stroking his nose with a PaperMate. Edward stared at him helplessly, saw his own reflection in a mirror (he had caught the sun), and then saw Lapôtre enter the lobby, cross the carpet, and walk out into the night. A car was heard to drive away.

"You're welcome."

Edward was leaning over the desk before the clerk could return to his book, a biography of Miss Judy Garland.

"The assistant manager? What about *him*?"

"I really can't leave the desk, sir."

"I'm not asking you to leave the desk."

"Then what *are* you asking me to do, sir?"

The clerk racked his glance up towards Edward, his eyes cold, subservience now a thing of the past.

"I just wanted to know," Edward replied, "I just wanted to know whether she had stayed here and in what room."

"If you give me her name again, I'll hand it into the office as soon as it opens."

"You mean—in the morning?"

"Yes, sir. In the morning. Seven a.m."

Edward stared at the clerk, hating him, hating his toupee, his pronunciation of the epithet "sir."

"Her name is Blanche," he said. "Blanche Asbury."

"And how do you—"

"A–S–B–U–R–Y. Asbury. It would have been about five or six years ago."

"We'll try and find out, sir, but you must understand we have had many hundreds of guests in the hotel over the years."

"I can't imagine why," Edward muttered, his face pink, fumbling the punch-line as always, and walked away towards the coolness of the terrace. The paw of a sleeping dog (poodle, pitiful creature) was trod on but Edward didn't apologize or delay his stride until he was outside. Nearby, tables were lit by candles in coloured-glass-holders and a few of the guests were sharing a late-night brandy or prefacing seductions. Daniel Azevedo was not there, but Mr. and Mrs. Parkins were, though Edward remained where he couldn't be seen. As he stood there, he could hear them talking and heard Mrs. Parkins say quite distinctly, "I wonder if there are *plaçements* in the restaurant?"

When Edward returned towards his room some time later (he had

Nightshade 150

visited the pool, had things to think about, sat on a canvas chair unaware of the *houngan* watching him behind the draperies of a stone Chloë), he paused beside the door to the Gable Suite—named in honour of the actor, a painted crown above the number. He needed someone to talk to and if it couldn't be Azevedo, then perhaps it might be Alice.

He was about to knock when he saw hanging from the door handle one of those quaint cards donated to guests on which to order their morning breakfast. It was pale blue and, according to the pencilled instructions, it would have been remiss for Edward, alas, to pursue his action. It clearly asked for two orange juices, two orders of scrambled eggs, one order of toast (diet, no doubt, rather than parsimony), English muffins, a coffee (male?), and a tea. Whose hand, Edward wondered, wrote each tick so neatly in its designated box? The crossed *seven* of 7:30, that finishing-school memento? What man would unscramble his eggs at that pleasant hour, sharing the salt? Silently, Edward turned and walked back to his room.

That night, neither Edward nor Amy slept until the early hours; nor did each undress immediately, unknown to each other, remaining in their chosen clothes in their individual rooms. Now and again Edward would walk out onto the balcony and stare at the road below and the lights of the city. He thought only of Daniel Azevedo, on the beach and at the villa, and of the two of them walking side by side. Edward tried to imagine where Azevedo might be. In bed, perhaps. Then he would return into his room and walk up and down. At one point, he considered taking a taxi and driving to the villa alone, just to walk in and say hello and see Azevedo's face turning towards him. He was even at the door of his room and stepping into the corridor when he stopped and returned quickly to his bed. "It would have been presumptuous of me. An intrusion, he said to himself and whenever he thought of that impulsive moment later, it embarrassed him. And so he remained in his room, on his bed. Mercifully, there were no more voices.

As for Amy, her feelings can be left to the reader. Though perhaps, on reflection, that is unfair. Let me just place you discreetly outside her half-open shutters in such a way that you may peer into the room. The light is on. You will now see that she has removed the hideous dress. It lies on a chair with her other garments. She is naked beneath the mosquito net, her back arched, her eyes closed, a radiator motif; but whatever fantasies she has now must remain her own. *It is sad but it is so.*

In a diary belonging to Edward Lytton, written on this date, there is no mention of Azevedo and one must assume that it was written in the early hours of the previous morning. On the relevant page can be found the following words: "I feel my mind is no longer at one with my body. This is not madness, nor what doctors may call schizophrenia. I am alert and my Faith, thank God, is undimmed. I am just prone to a fear that I cannot escape. It is not just a fear that makes me jump at shadows. If it were, I could, with God's help, overcome it. It is worse. It is what Montaigne wrote long ago: A fear that engenders terrible bewilderment. And I am alone. I am bewildered and I am alone, capable of only standing outside myself and watching my corpus enter the void. I try and console myself by saying that all this, all that is happening is just my imagination. And yet it cannot be so. Because I can see myself in the mirror, and there are lizards on the balcony."

Es inevitable la muerte del Papa:
Throw another dead dog into the ravine.

Part Five:
The Ninth Day

In the stumps of old trees where the hearts have rotted out/there are deep holes and dank pools where the rain gathers, and/if you ever put your hand down to see, you can wipe it in the/sharp grass till it bleeds, but you'll never want to eat with it again.

Hugh Sykes Davies

14

It would be appropriate to say that the next day it rained, that the clouds were black, and that a cold and terrifying wind blew across the country from the mountains and the sea beyond. But in truth, regrettably, there was nothing in the weather to indicate any hint of foreboding or of imminent tragedy; no dramatic stage directions to set the scene. It was in fact a fine day, one of the warmest of the season, the sky clear and blue as Wedgwood, with only a gouache of mists on the horizon and on the peaks of Gonave. It was also a holiday, celebrating a doubtful national event (*Pourboire publique*), and bells were rung in churches, schools were closed and children gathered in the squares to watch the parades or around the railings of the Palace to stare up at the balcony in the hope of seeing their President, Idol of the People, appearing with a dozen of his friends from the gym.

In his room, Edward awoke early, sunlight dazzling his eyes. He could hear maids chattering below his window in that now familiar Creole patois (*Pa pi mal*). Standing on his balcony he surveyed the town for a long time, as if memorizing it for future reference, until he heard a voice say, "Did you sleep well?"

It was unclear how long Amy herself had been standing viewing the same scene, and even now she did not look at him but remained quite still, a towelling robe wrapped around her, hand resting on neck. They were like two people in a drawing-room comedy, comparative strangers who had stepped out for a breath of fresh air, each in his individual way, counterpointing platitudes with the orchestra below.

"Not very. Did you?"

"Eventually. It was very humid."

"Was it?"

"Yes."

Edward thought about that then glanced at Amy. "How are you feeling?"

"I was thinking about that dress."

"Let us forget about it—"

"It could have been anybody's. A lot of people wear those dresses. . . ."

"Of course they do."

Amy smiled and was silent. They watched a jet take off, the light clear enough to read the name of the airline, watched it soar inland, turn, its undercarriage retracting before heading out to sea, probably to Miami.

"The doctor told me that it's not the first time people have complained of hearing voices."

"Why? Did Joan of Arc stay here?"

Amy suddenly laughed. "That's not funny, but it's funny."

"And Bernadette and—"

"Oh, Edward, don't spoil it."

"And Scrooge?"

"Scrooge?"

"Didn't he hear voices?"

"Did he?"

"I think so. Noises anyway."

"Well, it's something to do with the building. It's very badly designed."

"That's what *I* was told. That and the wine."

"What?"
Dainty hungers.
"What wine?"
"I was told—"
"By the doctor?"
"No."
Edward glanced away.
"I'm hungry," Amy said. "We've hardly eaten anything since yesterday lunchtime."
"Shall I order something?"
"No. *I'll* do it."
"It's no trouble."
"I can do it. Did you want anything? You must eat as well."
"Scrambled eggs."
Over breakfast in Amy's room, by the window, Edward said, "It doesn't matter any more. All those things. Now we're leaving."
While he was shaving, Amy appeared behind him in the mirror. She still hadn't dressed, having indicated that she wished to remain in the hotel for most of the morning in order to read and write some letters.
"We won't leave today, will we?" she asked.
Edward stared at her. "Why?"
"It's just that if we left too abruptly, it would be like . . . running away. Does that sound silly?"
"No."
A pause.
"Tomorrow then?" Edward said.
Amy smiled, picked up the Gillette, replaced it neatly on the side of the sink, then walked back into her room, closing the adjoining door. *We are friends again,* Edward thought.

The lobby of the hotel was crowded as guests and visitors prepared to take advantage of the weather and the opportunity to see Haiti at play. A few people were already drinking in the bar, margaritas and bloody marys to temper the mood, while the pianist commenced a repertoire of show stoppers with a bias towards *Top Hat*.

As Edward entered cautiously, fearing to see a familiar face, a man in shirtsleeves approached him and said, "Mr. Lytton?"

"Yes."

"We haven't met but my name is Hyssop, the assistant manager."

"Oh?"

"There was a message from you."

"Oh yes. Of course."

"You were inquiring about Miss Asbury."

"Yes."

"Well, I *do* remember her. She stayed here six years ago."

Edward stared at Hyssop, unsure of what to say. He suddenly felt awkward, standing in the centre of the lobby, wanting to move into an alcove.

"She was very popular," Hyssop continued. He smiled quickly, almost winked; then he saw Edward's expression and placed his hands behind his back and studied the floor. "She was with us for three months. I have it written down."

"Was she alone?" Edward asked.

"Alone? Well, she arrived here alone."

"What do you mean— 'She *arrived* here alone'?"

"Miss Asbury made friends very easily. I myself—"

Edward looked up quickly. Hyssop hesitated, almost shuffled his feet, then asked, "Are you a friend of hers, Mr. Lytton?"

"A relative."

"Oh. I see. Yes indeed. Well, you wanted to know her room. Is that right?"

"If's possible."

"I see no reason why not. She stayed in Room one-four-two. When she was here."

"One-four-two? Is that by chance the room above mine? Above the Valentino?"

"Oh no. No, it's on the ground floor, as you are. One-four-two is, let me see, next to the Gable Suite. Which actually is one-four-three."

"I see."

Hyssop nodded, glanced around as if anxious to leave, stepped back, then said, "If there's anything else, Mr. Lytton, please don't hesitate—"

"Yes, there is. They are ringing bells. Is this a Feast Day?"

In such a manner as this did the circumstances of this particular day begin. Edward attended Mass, not at the Cathedral but at a hillside church nearby, built out of wood and named after the Trinity. Small children of both sexes sang in the choir facing the congregation, and Edward prayed, face in hands, staying there till long after the service was over and hymn books and hassocks were being collected and placed in a cupboard. He prayed for Amy and for himself and for his parents. And he prayed for Blanche. She had never had a Requiem Mass, not officially, partly on the grounds that she was a suicide, her burial being more an act of embarrassment rather than a gesture of respect. It was something Edward had resented, but as Amy had said, "Blanche never believed in your God anyway. She had her own."

And she had, though Edward never found out which, despite his suspicions. Once, when they were walking alone along a bridle path set between winter corn and kale, he had asked Blanche what she believed in life. He remembered that she had stopped and looked at him (she was wearing a white anorak and a large-brimmed velvet hat) and replied, "I won't tell you the first, Edward, but I'll tell you the second. Sex. I believe in that very very much." Seeing Edward blush, she had laughed and taken his arm; but Edward wasn't surprised. He knew that she had had many lovers, had been with men since she was thirteen, had been discovered at fifteen in a tack room with an amateur jockey, and had said that she didn't care, didn't give a sod. Sex to her, she declared, was like eating, and she had no intention of starving or even of going on a diet. By the time she was seventeen, the number of her lovers was legendary, as well as the rumours that not all of them were men. Girls, it is said, had shared her bed (including a rather plain little thing who worked in the bakery), but Edward, naturally, never believed such scandal or even chose to listen to it. It was beyond his comprehension. Such things didn't exist. Girl's body against girl's body. That, of course, was before the incident in Tewkesbury.

On leaving the church, he saw Parkins sitting in the corner of a pew, arms folded, wearing a grey suit and a college tie.

"And how are you today?" Parkins asked.

"Fine," Edward replied, wondering whether to stop in the aisle.

"And how do you find Haiti?"

"We're leaving tomorrow."

"And why are you leaving tomorrow? Was it planned?"

"We don't want to stay here any more."

Parkins raised his head and studied Edward, then said quietly, "You mustn't let them know they've beaten you, Lytton. That's the secret. Never let the buggers know."

Edward hesitated, then walked out of the church into the sunlight, placing a coin in a box *pour les pauvres* and lighting a candle *pour les morts*.

Aware of his ability to lose his way, given the opportunity, Edward decided to walk back to the Dessalines by the same route that he had come. The path was now downhill, passing through the edge of a banana plantation, and then descending through the ruins of an abandoned village, built of stone two centuries earlier, but empty now— except for stray dogs, night creatures, and lizards. Much of the stonework was black, as if there had once been a fire that had been allowed to burn, either through neglect or design. On one or two walls, symbols were painted, curious designs that were repeated one above the other. Edward had seen them decorating posts by certain cross-roads and on the sleeves of the burnous worn by the *houngan*.

It was not a place to linger, even in daylight, but to hurry through quickly, thinking of other matters. Only one building remained intact, complete with a roof and a door, and when Edward had passed it earlier, he had noticed bars on the windows and had glanced in. He had thought he had seen things moving inside, in the darkness of the interior, semi-human creatures huddled one within the other, but he hadn't been sure. They could have been rats. Certainly he saw eyes and heard a scuffling. Passing it on the return journey (he had forgotten the building until he encountered it turning a corner) he kept at a distance from the window, though unable to look away. Nevertheless, his footsteps must have announced his arrival, for he heard the scuffling again, and above it a kind of indefinable sliding, scraping, as if something living was dragging itself with great difficulty over damp earth.

Edward stopped (the unknown no longer a cause for panic; such, at least, had been achieved) and slowly approached the rusted bars of the window and the blackness within. The noises suddenly stopped, and he sensed that he was being observed.

"Hello?" Edward said, quite calmly, as if entering a *salon* where he was expected.

There was no reply, merely a long deep sigh of great sadness, and then something was placed between the bars into the light. At first Edward thought it was a stump of charred wood or a tube of rubber, hacked from a tire. It was only when he moved closer to it that he saw that it was moving, and that it had once been a hand. He heard the sigh once more but this time it evoked an even greater sadness, since it was almost petulant in tone, like a child who has been told that he has to go to bed early.

"Don't touch it," a voice said behind him.

Edward turned and saw Azevedo.

"The village used to harbour lepers, but now only these are left."

Edward glanced back at the window, heard the sigh repeated, then walked away, following Azevedo until they were standing amid blossoms of bougainvillaea looking down at the roof of the hotel. Two people in clean white shirts and shorts were playing tennis, rather badly, on a court below.

"I saw you go past here earlier, Edward," Azevedo said. "I hoped you would come back."

"Poor creatures," Edward said.

"Who? Those two down there?"

"Does no one care about them?"

"Not any more. They're in the wrong century."

The chance encounter with Azevedo did not unduly surprise Edward. It had seemed impossible that he would not meet him again; not by arrangement (twice, there had been definite appointments, and twice, one or the other had not appeared) but in a manner such as this, appearing suddenly and quite naturally since that first day at Revenants. *It is because he has enemies,* Edward thought, flattered by the confidence, *he has to be careful.*

"I'm leaving Haiti, Edward. I wanted to see you to tell you that."

This was said quite unemotionally. A simple statement of fact, and as such Edward was startled. He hadn't expected it. It was going to be *he* who was going to announce his departure.

"Leaving? When?"

"Tonight. Before the day's over."

"Oh, I see."

There was a pause and Edward looked away. He suddenly realized that he would never see Azevedo again. "Oh, I see," he repeated, hating the absurd phrase. Below, one of the tennis players could be heard shouting and then was seen running towards the net.

"Is it because of . . . of your enemies?" he asked.

Azevedo didn't reply but lit a cigarette.

"I would have told you last night," he said finally, "but you didn't arrive."

"Arrive?" Edward asked, startled. "We waited—"

"I thought you would come and see me."

"Well, I wanted to but—"

"We could have talked. You and I. Played backgammon. Drunk some wine."

"I was going to—" Edward began to stammer. What had he done wrong?

"There were so many things I wanted to say, Edward. Now, it's too late."

"No—of course it isn't. We could talk now. I'm sorry about last night but—"

"I have things to do."

Azevedo turned and looked at Edward, and said, "As *you* always have 'things to do.' "

Edward was stunned. "You must understand, it wasn't my fault about last night. Amy was upset. She suffers from hallucinations."

But Azevedo was no longer listening. He was walking away down the hill, towards the village.

"Wait a minute," Edward called out, running after him. "Please believe me. I didn't think. It was all so casual. You said—"

Azevedo didn't stop. He was now walking past a ruined building that had once been a stable. Boxes could be seen, an iron manger still bolted to the remains of a wall.

"Daniel?" Edward shouted.

Azevedo stopped and turned around. "I never thought you would disappoint me, Edward. Not like those Americans."

"I never meant to disappoint you. I never meant that. I waited. I didn't know that you . . ." And then: "I'm sorry."

There was nothing more to say. It seemed to Edward that it was madness that it should finish like this, in some kind of absurd misunderstanding. But Azevedo was already fifty yards away, moving towards the plantation. Even as Edward ran after him, stumbling, then running on, he could only see the other man's silhouette, partly hidden by trees.

"How will you leave?" Edward called out. "Will you be all right?"

"I have my own means."

"Wouldn't you want any help?"

There was no answer. Edward could see a glimpse of an arm, a shoulder, the collar of the white silk shirt, and then Azevedo was suddenly standing very close in a clearing so that one could reach out and touch him. If one so wished.

It was agreed by the doctor that Amy was much better and that there was no further cause for alarm. She had eaten breakfast and then taken tea and cakes at eleven o'clock on the terrace, sitting at the centre table and listening to the piano, an unread book by the side of her plate. Lapôtre had kissed her hand.

Later, she was seen walking in the gardens alone, wearing her white dress, walking slowly, as if preoccupied, now and then stopping to touch the base of a statue or a leaf or stare up towards the hills around Kenscoff, as if absorbing everything around her. When she finally returned to the hotel, it was almost noon. She inquired about Edward, but he hadn't returned. When he did return, an hour later, Amy was sitting by the pianist, a glass of Bacardi by her side, vamping the lower register as they improvised a parlour song.

"Amy?" Edward said quietly, standing near her.

"Oh, hello. Listen—do you recognize it?"

"Amy?"

"Ssshh. Watch." And then to the pianist, "Right. From the top. Isn't that what you say? Edward—listen."

But Edward had turned and walked out of the lobby. His absence was not noticed, nor even missed, until the song had been played twice more and one or two onlookers had applauded.

"She reminds me of that whore, Blanche Asbury," Hyssop said. "She used to play that. Do you remember?"

Edward remained in his room until Amy returned, opening the door and saying, "We were looking for you. Aren't you having lunch? We're eating with those people called Parkins. *À quatre* as his wife says. He said he saw you in church. God, he's boring, isn't he? All those questions. Ooops, too much rum."

"I saw Azevedo," Edward said, keeping his back to her, carefully placing a pair of shoes into a suitcase. "He's leaving Haiti tonight. He told me to tell you."

Amy stared across the room for a moment, then said, "Oh well."

Nothing more was said, nor was Azevedo mentioned again by either husband or wife. Amy merely went into her own room and closed the partition door, a bath was heard being filled, and then finally she reappeared wearing the pale blue cotton shirt she had worn on the day they had visited the sulphur mines and mineral springs of Revenants. On a toe of her left foot was a strip of Band-Aid. The fourth button of her shirt was undone, probably by accident.

Edward hadn't moved but was still standing by the bed, before the open suitcase. He appeared very calm, very relaxed. It was as if Amy was seeing him for the first time, had entered a room and seen a man standing there.

"The holiday was worthwhile after all. As it had to be," was all that Edward said.

He decided against lunch in the restaurant, saying that he couldn't bear the company of Parkins and that he had letters to write. He would eat alone in his room. In fact, only one letter was written and that was addressed to his wife, Amy. It was unfinished and by the way it was written, the words had obviously been difficult to set down. What remains are a few disjointed sentences such as: *I understand now about Tewkesbury. About you and Blanche. I want to tell you that.* And then two lines rendered unreadable (the word *love* can be deciphered), followed by the phrase *I didn't realize before that such things were possible.* This is repeated and then the rather curious use of the word *revenge,* though it is unclear to whom or what this refers. The last legible paragraph tells Amy that he loves her, quite simply and with great tenderness. *When we return to England,* it concludes, *our marriage will begin as if the last few months had never happened. Forgive me, Amy* prefaces a further avowal of love. The letter now ends unsigned, though it is apparent that something further was to be written, something that Edward could not say to Amy face-to-face. No matter, for she never read the letter, nor even knew of its existence. It remained in Edward's pocket, hidden from the world as always.

After finishing his lunch (*salade niçoise*), Edward called the desk and rebooked the airline tickets for the next morning. He was also informed that there was a package waiting for him, and that it would be sent to his room. Edward waited on the balcony, listening to the music from the loudspeakers in the nearby stadium, the arc lights draped in the red and black flags of Haiti. Below him, in the park of the hotel, watered by sprinklers, he saw a man standing watching him, saw him gesture (a slanting of the hand at chest level, as if drawing an imaginary line parallel to the ground); then the man, whom he now recognized as the *houngan,* walked away towards a group of Tontons, who were laughing, pistols at their belts. *They'll never catch him now,* Edward thought.

There was a knock on the door and a bellboy entered and handed Edward the package. He recognized it as a folder of photographs, sent from the Iron Market.

"Is there anything to pay?" he asked.

The bellboy shrugged and then left.

Opening the folder, Edward saw that only four photographs had been printed out of thirty-six. Each one was of Amy taken before they left England, standing on the lawn of their house, entering a car. All the other pictures, as the negatives showed, were black. Surprisingly, Edward showed no annoyance since he never prided himself on being an efficient photographer. He assumed that the mistake was his own (he had forgotten to remove the lens' cap, too much exposure, and such like mishaps) and accepted the fact that there was now no pictorial record of the holiday as fortuitous. It was as it should be.

Later, in the restaurant, he drank coffee and brandy with Parkins, his wife, and Amy, though declined to accompany them on a tour of the city "to see what the nignogs were up to."

"There is safety *en masse,*" said Mrs. Parkins. Her first name, it was learned, was Henrietta, the daughter of an English peer of indeterminate habits (the Stork Room, Annabel's, week-ends avoiding the press, that kind of thing), who had married Parkins because she was bored, and there was a blank date in her diary. Her life was devoted to such sweet foibles as choosing the right colour for the kitchen, overfeeding her children, and attending masked balls for Famine Relief.

"No, I think I've seen as much of Haiti as I wish," Edward said, gazing at Amy, who was sitting overlooking the steps, remote, as if she belonged somewhere else.

"And are you disappointed?" Parkins asked.

"Not any more."

"But your wife wishes to come with us. She said so."

Edward looked at Amy but she made no reaction. He suddenly wanted to touch her, the triangle of bare skin beneath her neck, the top buttons of her shirt undone. For a moment, he was in that other restaurant on that other island, eating *accra chou*. It was so overpowering, this transposition in time that he said it out loud before realizing it.

"*Déjà vu,*" said Mrs. Parkins.

"Yes. I suppose that's what it is."

A taxi was ordered and Edward stood on the steps as Parkins and his wife walked towards the car. Amy didn't follow them immediately, but stopped and walked back towards Edward, her hands together, one within the other.

"Do you mind, Edward?"

"No. Of course not. I've got a headache. Probably a combination of Parkins and the brandy."

"What will you do?"

"Oh, read a book. Go for a walk. You know."

Edward smiled and studied her: "Maybe try and finish that biography of Melbourne once and for all."

Amy nodded but didn't move, apparently reluctant to leave. Behind her, Parkins was calling out her name. And then she looked up and said, "I've never deceived you, Edward. Not in the way you said. I've never played games."

It seemed a startling thing for her to say at that precise moment, and Edward laughed self-consciously and said something like, "Oh, don't be silly. It's all forgotten," and words to that effect, until he heard Parkins shout, "Come on, Amy, or we'll lose the taxi."

"You'd better go," Edward said.

"Are you sure you'll be all right? You won't be bored?"

"No. I'll be all right."

"There are a couple of paperbacks in my room if you get tired of the Melbourne."

"I'll see how I feel."

Amy looked at him and then said, "There are some aspirins by my bed. For your headache. If you need them."

These words of maternal consideration, trivial as they may seem, are exact to the letter. There is nothing sinister to be read in them. It is just that they are the last words that were ever exchanged between Edward and Amy, and as such they deserve to be recorded just as they stand.

At seven o'clock, the Parkinses returned to the hotel. They were alone.

15 At first, Edward was not unduly concerned. He had spent the afternoon by himself, not in his room, but sitting beneath an ash tree, shunning the crowds, and thinking of England. In particular, of the English countryside, retracing favourite walks in Gloucestershire or on the Malvern Hills, retracing each step in detail, as if deliberately eliminating any thoughts of Haiti, of the holiday and what had happened in these past few days.

At one point he thought he saw Alice walking in the shadow of a pergola, but he didn't call out her name, even though she was alone, but watched her from his vantage point until she had gone. Immediately, he began to look for her, suddenly wanting to be with her, attempting to banish the absurd rigours he had clamped to his character in the past. *I am forty years old and I have wasted my life. I have almost killed my senses,* he had told Azevedo—until he was reassured that it wasn't yet too late. Alice, however, was nowhere to be seen. The opportunity had been missed, and so Edward returned to the bench beneath the tree and began to daydream. In his imagination he saw two people who were naked and one-dimensional, as if cut out of a child's book, cardboard tabs on arms and legs, waiting to be clothed by a selection of garments depicted on an adjacent page. A white silk shirt for the man, for example, or that hat to cover the girl's red hair.

As it grew later and he became aware that he was hungry, Edward put aside such warm diversions and strolled back to the hotel. It was there that he saw Parkins, sitting at the bar with his wife, detailing the story of the diva Caviglia, stabbed to death behind a snowdrift by a lunatic admirer. Edward listened, mostly out of politeness, and accepted a drink. He noticed that the portrait of Pheobe Stanley had been removed, and was pleased about that. He had never liked the picture, considering that not only was it badly composed but that the subject of the painting looked totally heartless.

"Has Amy gone to her room?" he asked finally in a lapse in conversation.

"Amy?" Parkins asked. "I have no idea. Why? When did she come back?"

"Why ask me?" Edward said and laughed.

"I thought you might have seen her arrive."

"Now why should I have done that?" Edward asked and laughed again.

"Well, she didn't come back with us."

"Amy didn't?"

"No, she didn't."

Edward looked at both husband and wife—the latter now asking for a *soupçon* of vermouth in her martini—then said casually, "I assumed—"

"And *I* assumed also. But your wife left us after we arrived at the museum. She said she wanted to tour on her own."

"Just like Amy."

"And why is that?"

"She can be very unpredictable. Where did she go?"

"She didn't say."

"She didn't say," repeated Henrietta.

"She wasn't ill?"

Nightshade   170

"A little agitated perhaps. No," Parkins added quickly. "She seemed quite determined to go her own way. No, not agitated at all."

"I see."

Silence, and Edward smiled and said, "Probably wanted to go swimming."

"Do you think so?"

"Well, she swims, doesn't she? You saw her at the beach on the other island."

Parkins frowned, considered this, then shook his head.

"No. Did we?" he asked.

"At the barbecue," Edward said. "You mentioned you saw Amy swimming. You admired how well—"

"No. No. It was someone else."

"But you said—"

"Couldn't have been. Different woman altogether. Your wife is fair."

"Mousy."

"And the woman I saw was quite different. My mistake."

"Are you sure?"

"Of course. We saw a woman we thought was Amy, but now that we've met her, we were wrong. Does it matter?"

"No. Of course not," Edward replied.

Amy was right, he thought. *She did not deceive me.*

"Doesn't matter at all."

Parkins and his wife turned away and began to whisper to each other, as if Edward no longer existed. He tried to interrupt but heard only a sibilant rustling, like taffeta under crinoline; then the couple stood up and walked away. He heard Henrietta Parkins say, *"Oui, mais c'est moi qui en souffre,"* and then she stopped to talk to Lapôtre and walked out of the lobby.

As was stated, Edward was not at first unduly worried about Amy's absence. He assumed she had taken the opportunity to see the last of Haiti before returning to England.

Until it grew dark.

And there was still no sign of her.

She was certainly not in her room, because he had looked there, ostensibly to collect the aspirins by her bedside. He had noticed that she had not yet packed, though her suitcase had been taken from a cupboard and placed on a rack, either to be filled or for an object to be removed. Opening it, he saw a small plastic folder (a familiar possession), designed to contain photographs and other bric-à-brac. There was a snapshot of Edward, taken, as he recalled, outside the Public Library in Cheltenham, and another of a girl in white, whom he recognized as Blanche. She was no more than twelve years old, squinting at the sun, laughing. On the back, written in ink, were the words, "Ramsgate. April 30." Another photograph of Edward, a sepia study of Carole Lombard, a newspaper drawing of a pair of shoes. Other objects to be picked up and replaced in the red silk lining: an oyster shell, a book of hymns, a lock of black hair, a bar of soap, a feather. As Edward was studying each article, something entered the room behind him and stood in the recess of the wardrobe, then moved to the bed and turned down a sheet and rearranged the mosquito net.

"I'd rather you didn't smoke in here," Edward said.

By nine o'clock, Edward feared that Amy would not return. That something might have happened to her. He needed advice, someone who knew the island. In the corridor, he knocked on the door of the Gable Suite and was surprised to see Henrietta Parkins opening it and saying:

"Isn't this place extraordinary? Isn't everything *de trop*?"

Edward stared at her, glanced back at the door, back into the room, and stammered, "Is this your room?"

"Yes. Who's Gable? Not the lovely man in *Gone With the Wind*?"

"I've made a mistake."

"Have you? Oh dear."

"No. I'm sorry. The hotel is very confusing. I thought someone else was staying in this suit—*suite*."

"Just us. *Comme il faut. Chez nous.*"

In a corner of the room, Edward could see a television screen, a report of the 20,000-ton freighter *Anita* that had disappeared off Bermuda.

"Come in. Come in, Edward."

Henrietta was holding a glass of wine in her right hand.

"No. I'm looking for—"

"Looking for?"

"Looking for Amy. My wife."

"Do you mean she hasn't returned?"

"No. Well, not yet."

"Oh, don't worry. Come in."

"No. Thank you."

Edward stared at the door again, then he said, "Were you here last night?"

"Yes. What an extraordinary question. *Comme il faut.*"

"Excuse me, but did you order scrambled eggs for breakfast?"

Henrietta stared at him, then laughed and added, "Muffins as well."

"I've made a mistake," Edward said. "It must be another room. All doors look the same."

"But don't leave us, *Edouard. Pas maintenant.*"

"I'm sorry. Perhaps later."

"Don't worry," Parkins called out, suddenly appearing behind his wife, shaving-soap under his chin. "Amy can look after herself."

"Yes."

"She was quite determined."

"Yes."

"There's some wine."

In the lobby there was no news. Edward had asked discreetly at the desk, since he didn't want to "make a fuss," and had then walked out onto the steps, conscious of the laughter and the sounds of people still celebrating the holiday. In the sky, there were fireworks.

As he stood there, he sensed someone approach him, and then Alice was beside him, leaning back against a pillar.

"Hello," she said.

Edward looked at her but didn't answer.

"What's the matter?" she asked. "Too much of that wine again?"

"No."

Alice nodded as if understanding, and was about to move away when Edward said, "Don't go."

Alice hesitated, unsure.

"I wanted to talk to you earlier," Edward continued, "but I couldn't find your room. I thought you were in the Gable Suite."

"No. Next door."

"It's just . . ."

Edward stopped, and then he said, "It's Amy. She hasn't returned."

"Returned? Returned from where?"

"I don't know. She went out on her own. I mean, a woman alone in this place . . . These people . . ."

"Did she say when she'd be back?"

"No. But—"

"I'm sure she's all right. Maybe she's just visiting a friend. Does she have any friends here?"

"No," Edward replied, and then he stared at Alice and said "No" again. *I saw Azevedo. He's leaving Haiti tonight. He told me to tell you.*

"She doesn't make friends."

Oh well.

"Perhaps you could call the police?" Alice suggested.

He has enemies.

"No," Edward said. "We needn't bother about that. She'll be all right."

Edward then smiled and reached out to take Alice's hand, but stopped and looked away.

"Thank you," he said quietly, almost bowed, then walked down the steps onto the driveway. He heard someone, an American, greet him and comment on the weather, and Edward replied that it was indeed a fine evening, and continued walking without looking back.

In the taxi to Kenscoff he burst into tears, hiding his face, pressing it against the window. "It was going to be the happiest of times," he said to himself, and then muttered something absurd, something maudlin and apologized to the driver.

It was in these circumstances that Edward Lytton visited Villa Azevedo for the second time.

The taxi was now high in the mountains, driving through the darkness without incident. It had left the main road and turned south and onto a lane through a pine forest. Edward, peering through the window, vainly tried to recognize a landmark, and then entrusted the journey to the driver. At one point he thought he saw a man picked out by the headlights, and for a moment he was convinced it was Azevedo. The man seemed to be waving to him almost frantically, as if in warning, and Edward called out to the driver to stop. But either the request was not heard, or was ignored, for the taxi continued and by that time the figure had gone. There was only the night, Spanish moss clinging to cypresses and the incessant chatter of insects.

"Didn't you see that man?" Edward asked. *"Cet homme-là."*
"Non. Pas de tout."

After ten minutes, the taxi finally stopped. It was near a stone shed (*houmfort*), and drums could be heard. Through an open door, shapes could be seen dancing like chickens, fingertips on knees, and women in white were sitting very still around a central pillar.

"*Pourquoi ici?*" Edward asked, startled, as the driver switched off the engine and got out of the car. There was no reply, simply a raising of the shoulders and a hand extended for money. For reasons unknown, Edward was abandoned, and he knew that argument was useless. Cautious not to ask specifically for the villa, he questioned the direction to Kenscoff and was rewarded with a mere gesture into the darkness and nothing more. The driver then walked towards the shed and stood silhouetted for a moment, while talking to another man who had appeared from within. Both men then looked towards Edward, and he heard the drums stop—not completely, but just a solitary tapping, fingers on buckskin. Faces were seen and children began to emerge through the narrow opening like small black creatures disturbed from hibernation and moving towards something they might want to devour.

"Oh my God, don't they know I can't swim?" Edward shouted, and then he began to run, as if the poor fool hadn't suffered enough. It is difficult to calculate how long he ran, and for the purposes of this tale it is not important to detail each tree, each stumbling block in the undergrowth. It need only be said that, in time, Edward realized that there was no sound of pursuit (at least none that he could hear), and that eventually a path was found that opened into a track large enough for a vehicle, and that he soon emerged onto a height from which he could see not only the lights of Port-au-Prince but also the villa of Daniel Azevedo. It was no more than fifty yards away, and he could see, despite the darkness, that all the shutters were closed except one, the shutter appended to the third bedroom. A light was visible, flickering within the room, possibly from a candle or a small oil-lamp. There was the gentle movement of shadows.

It was at this moment, as Edward approached the house, that he became aware of the silence. This is not to say that there was no noise at all (bats are very objective mammals) but that there was simply a controlled stillness, as when one holds one's breath or, more accurately, enters into a state of meditation. Of suspension. The mind selects, and whether induced naturally or unnaturally (by drugs, say), it can, if successful, reach the apogee of nothingness. In a sense, it is a blissful negation, and it is what Edward experienced as he stood in the library looking at familiar objects, the backgammon board set out for yet another game. There was a sense of ultimate peace, almost divine, that he had rarely known before, and as such it produced once again this sense of detachment from himself. He noticed details: inanimate objects breathed a life, seemed to move. Time became nonexistent. The sensation was, if you wish, mystical.

Edward stood in the room for perhaps half an hour. He had selected a book at random from the bookshelf and had opened it out to the bookplate. He had seen the design before. It was this:

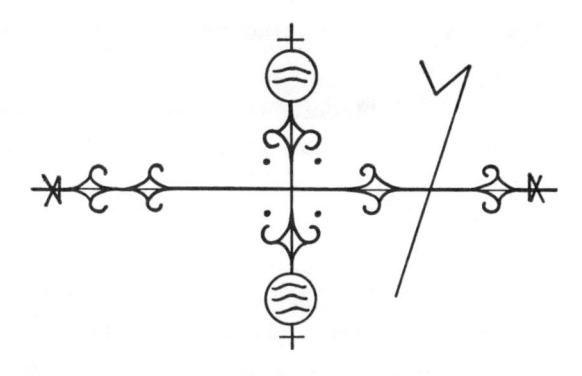

Underneath were the words *EX LIBRIS DANIEL AZEVEDO* etched in fine copperplate. As Edward was about to replace the book, he heard a sound, familiar but unrecognizable. It was from above him, from the third bedroom, and he could only define it as the disturbance of a branch on a tree; a creaking and then a nuzzling. Odd, these associations of the mind.

"I will go and see," Edward said out loud, as if addressing a nervous companion. "I will go and see what it may be."

This action required him to leave the library and enter the darkness of the corridor, unaided by moonlight, and then up the main stairs, conscious of a lizard, the dampness of a wall. He could see the lighted room since the door was partially open, and then his hand was on the panelled wood itself and was pushing it slowly forward creating a series of rectangles, each one an inch wider than the last until a complete chair was observed, part of a mirror, then all of the mirror; and then the rectangle embraced the window and the nuzzling hesitated; there was a silence, a bed came into view and something scampered into a corner, shivering. *A rat,* Edward thought. *Nothing more.* And then standing in the bedroom he looked at the unmade bed, the rumple of warm sheets, a statue of Grande Erzulie above it all. Lowering his hand slowly over the bed he touched the wetness, and then moved his fingers to the light and turned off the lamp. As he did so, he looked out of the window and saw the boys huddled by a tree, standing near the bougainvillaea. He could see their faces quite clearly reflected in the light of the torches in their hands.

It will burn quite easily, Edward thought. *The flames will be seen for miles.*

Turning away, he drew the curtains and walked back across the room, his hand reaching out in the darkness, his fingers suddenly touching a mouth.

My Darling Amy
We are now one. You and I. I am your body. You are my spirit. Perhaps you will never understand this because you have never been loved as I have been loved. There is nothing else that matters. The loving. Life saddens me now, for I have left him for you. Seek him out. You have his name. Love him as I did. There are other worlds, dear Amy dear Amy. There is another life, dear Amy. Pray for me.
            Sleep in my cot, dear Amy.
Save me, dear Amy
    Je t'aime. Je t'adore.
        Blanche

It was the mouth and face of a man.

"So Azevedo chose *you,*" a voice said.

"Who is this?" Edward replied, hands seeking the lamp, fumbling, drawing back the curtains to let in light.

"No," the voice continued. "It couldn't be you. It is the ninth day. He must have chosen someone else."

Edward could now see the *houngan.* He was wearing a red burnous and there were metal bracelets on each wrist.

"What are you saying to me?" Edward asked. "Ninth day? Ninth day since when?"

"Then it is your wife," the *houngan* said and walked into the corridor. "But then it had to be."

He could be heard descending the staircase, and after a moment there was music as a gramophone was wound up below. The record was scratched but recognizable. It was a classic by Bix Beiderbecke, the cornet hard and fast. The children outside could obviously hear it, because they were grinning and jumping up and down on the lawn. *She has taken the hat,* Edward thought. *It is not on the chair.*

In the hallway, Edward took hold of the *houngan*'s sleeve, pulling him around.

"Tell me where Azevedo is. Tell me that."

"I don't know, Monsieur Lytton. But it doesn't matter now."

Edward suddenly smiled and stood back.

"Then he has escaped you, hasn't he? He told me you were his enemy."

Jean-Dantor turned and said, "Did you love him as well, Monsieur Lytton? As your wife does?"

It is possible that Edward was about to strike the *houngan* since he raised his hand, but then moved away and pressed himself against the wall. Something ran across his hair.

"Azevedo is like an eel," the *houngan* said quietly. "An eel, as you know, has a fondness for human flesh. It enters a drowned body through the eyes. Azevedo is like that."

"Amy has not drowned," Edward replied defiantly.

"She is drowning, Monsieur Lytton. I knew that when I first saw her."

A silence; then Edward said, "Where can I find him? Can't you tell me that?"

"No. I never saw him. Only you and your wife saw him. And those Americans. I assume they were coming here."

Edward made no reaction.

"He has destroyed four people at least, Monsieur Lytton. Why not another?"

Outside, two of the children, who were naked, could be seen sitting on the shoulders of two others, a boy and a girl. In the torchlight, one of them, the boy, seemed almost fair. Like a European. He was no more than six years old, if that. The features were not unfamiliar.

In the library, Edward sat before the backgammon board and slid a counter into a corner. Leaning back he could see the photograph frame. Picking it up, he reached out to remove the back cover to expose the picture. Then he stopped. *No. It doesn't matter now.* And he placed it back in its position. It will burn with the rest.

The book was still open where he had left it. It was, as it happened, a pilot's handbook. The last entry, written nine days before, read *Today we leave for Revenants.*

It was now past midnight. Edward looked at the room, touched the chair. He could smell smoke and hear the crackling of flames, wood moving into wood. Then he picked up a glass that had once been held and touched by Azevedo, and this he kept. Nothing else. It seemed, tragically, the only thing he dared to take.

As he left, the villa was on fire. The taxi-driver was waiting, saying that Jean-Dantor had asked him to remain to drive Edward back to the hotel.

"I will find Amy," Edward said.

And he did.

16 The wreckage of the Cessna was found at the base of the mountain, close to the road that leads to Cap Haïtien in the north. Villagers from a nearby *coumbite* had confirmed that the plane (green and white) had been flying no more than three hundred feet above the jungle, travelling parallel to the ground, before entering the side of the mountain itself without altering altitude. It was said by some that it didn't even try.

By the time Edward arrived, driven there by the police from the hotel, flares had already been set up and spotlights from the rescue vehicles. He saw the mountain first, and then, raising his head, the Citadel set on the peak—the fortress built by Henri Christophe against the French—now in silhouette above it all. Battlements could be seen. Stepping out of the car, Edward became conscious of the noise and the suppressed excitement that accompanies such events. He noticed a starboard wing placed delicately in the earth like a surfboard, a blade of the propeller embedded in a tree; the sound of frogs; a group of women running into the darkness carrying a leather-covered chair, its seat-belts flapping around their legs; an ashtray; the body of Amy; a wheel that had slid along its strut like a button on a needle.

As he was led into the centre of the light he heard Lapôtre say, "This is the fifth accident like this in two years. It is either a mountain or the sea. Usually the sea."

And then Parkins said, "The filthy bastards. Sue them for all they have."

"Please don't say that again," Edward said angrily, and then he apologized.

Standing by the cabin, he stared at Amy's face. She was still sitting strapped into one of the two rear seats (the aisle), her head turned and looking to her left, not out of the window exactly but towards the adjacent seat, her mouth open, almost as if she was involved in a private conversation that she didn't want anyone else to hear. On her lap she was holding the straw hat very tightly.

"Yes, that is Amy. That is my wife," Edward said.

There was a series of flashes as two men took photographs, one of them asking Edward, in French, to stand just a little to his left.

"It should have been me," Edward said out loud.

His attention was then distracted by something that was happening nearby, in the undergrowth. He had been aware of the *houngan* when he arrived, but now he found himself watching as Jean-Dantor seemed to kneel, then lie down on an object that was on the ground. It was a corpse. The *houngan* was holding a rattle in his hand and shaking it, and then he began to whisper in the corpse's ear, calling out a name. This continued for some time, watched in awe by all those around him. A few of the women had joined in the chant and seemed to be in a trance, until, suddenly, the corpse shuddered and slowly raised its head, as if wanting to be kissed before dropping back to the ground as the *houngan* screamed, a horrific shout of joy, almost of orgasm, then collapsed back onto the dead body, soothing it with words that couldn't be heard.

"The ceremony is called *désunnin*," Lapôtre said, standing beside Edward. "He is now with the *loa*."

"Who is?" Edward asked, then suddenly ran forward, aware of hands trying to stop him. Reaching the *houngan,* he looked down and saw beneath him the black face of a man of fifty, the head almost bald.

Nightshade   182

"It is the pilot," Jean-Dantor said, standing up. "His name is Gommier. That was his plane. He used to fly every day from Pétionville to Cap Haïtien taking tourists or others who hired him. It was said he could fly the route wearing a blindfold. That is his father standing over there. The man in the blue-checked shirt."

Edward made no comment, then turned to walk away.

"Do you still believe it is nonsense, Monsieur Lytton?" the *houngan* asked.

"I don't know. I don't know any more."

"Still the doubting Thomas?"

Edward stared at the empty seat in the Cessna, its back adjusted to be on the level with that occupied by Amy, a pillow on the headrest indicating an impression.

"You will not see Azevedo again. Not any more," he heard the *houngan* say.

Though the area was searched till noon the next day, no other bodies—apart from those of the pilot and Amy Lytton—were found.

In the car back to the hotel, Edward sat with Parkins, irritated by the man's presence but grateful, nonetheless, for his gesture of sympathy. There is very little one can talk about in a situation like this and Edward felt almost embarrassed, wanting to apologize for being such a nuisance.

"I blame myself," Parkins said. "We should have looked after her yesterday."

"No, it wasn't your fault."

"But if only she had mentioned she had wanted to visit the Citadel. It's one of the things Henrietta and I had planned as well. We could have gone with her—"

Parkins stopped and laughed nervously.

"Oh, my God."

There was a silence, and then Edward said after a moment, "I don't think she was going to the Citadel. She took her passport. Do you need a passport to go there?"

"Her passport?"

"It was in her bag."

Parkins suddenly stared at Edward, studying him, wanting to ask more, but reluctantly changed his mind.

"What a rotten way to end a holiday," he said instead, and then added, taking out a panatela, "Do you mind if I smoke?"

The car was now approaching the capital, following the same route from the airport. Soon they would see the Cathedral.

"And what will you do now?" Parkins asked.

"Go back to England, I suppose."

"And when will you leave?"

"They said there's no reason for me to stay—once the formalities are over. They will send Amy back as soon as possible. Apparently, they prefer the coffin to travel as freight rather than on a passenger plane. I can understand that, in a way."

"Yes. Nothing worse than looking out of the window before take-off and seeing . . . Are you sure you don't mind if I smoke?"

"No. I don't mind."

Passing a restaurant, Edward watched as a man unlocked shutters on the main windows, while nearby a waiter set out tables and chairs ready for the day. It was now morning.

"All I can say," Parkins muttered, "is that *we* won't be sorry to leave this place. It's damn uncivilized if you ask me. Henrietta was reading these books all about voodoo and evil spirits. Good God, do they really expect me to believe nonsense like that?"

"Supposing you loved someone," Edward said quietly, "and you knew that that someone intended to kill you."

"Is this a game?"

"And yet no one can help you. They cannot help you because no one knows that your murderer exists. Has an existence. . . ."

"What?"

"Except perhaps one other person. A rival."

"It is a game. Say it again. Supposing what . . . ?"

"It was one of Amy's games."

Parkins stared at Edward, then laughed nervously, and then was silent. Finally, he replied, "I never knew your wife very well," simply for want of anything else to say.

When the car arrived at the hotel, some of the guests were already sitting on the terrace waiting for breakfast. Edward could see faces looking at him as he was driven up the main driveway, one or two people in the garden whispering, then looking away. He felt self-conscious, something to be avoided. Ignoring them, he stepped out of the car, and as he did so he looked up, over the roof of the car, gazing idly towards the balconies, most of which had canopies pulled down against the morning sun.

"There's someone outside Amy's room," he said.

"Wha'? Wadje say?" Parkins asked.

"A woman. She's gone now."

"Probably a maid."

"No. It wasn't a maid."

Parkins looked at Edward then followed his gaze. "Which balcony are you talking about?"

"That one. Just to the left of the tallest palm tree."

"Left of the tallest palm tree? But I thought you were in the Valentino Suite?"

"We are. I am."

"But that's not the Valentino. That's mine. I recognize Henrietta's bathing costume. And that's her yellow towel."

"We had *two* balconies."

"Even so. You're miles from us."

Edward stared at the hotel, now suddenly familiar with its design, and nodded. *She was right about that too.*

"Look, Edward," Parkins said, taking his arm. "If there's anything we can do, just ask. I wouldn't entrust a sod to these nignogs. The best thing they can do is get us a drink."

In the bar, Edward allowed himself to be bought a brandy. He felt emotionless, a deadness behind the eyes, but he knew that this was a temporary state. In time the shock would hit him, as it happened after

185 The Ninth Day

the death of Blanche. And yet in his mind he kept repeating, *It should have been me. Why wasn't it?* And it was this that brought the remorse, unapparent as it was to the observer.

Henrietta had joined her husband and they both sat down on barstools beside him, sipping silently at their drinks, Henrietta having ordered a Campari. Edward stared at them through the bar mirror, watching them mouthing familiar platitudes of concern, hating them both, and almost smiling at the absurdity of their appearance, the pathetic attempt to wear "respectful attire" that was making them sweat, Parkins' pitiful baby-pink hands.

Abandoning them he walked to the desk to send a telegram to Amy's parents. As he asked for the form, he heard Parkins whisper to his wife:

"She was leaving him. She was running away."

Edward paid no attention but wrote, AMY DEAD; then he crossed this out and wrote instead, BAD NEWS STOP AM RETURNING ALONE STOP EDWARD.

At ten o'clock, police and other officials arrived, statements were taken, and certificates were exchanged. There was some confusion about the actual charter of the Cessna, since no official announcement had been made by Gommier, the pilot. However, the police were well aware that the plane was often used for illegal flights from a private airfield, and they accepted it as that. Moreover, since the pilot was dead, there seemed no need to pursue the matter.

"Have you any reason why your wife was on the plane?" someone asked.

Edward looked up at a police officer, who was wearing dark glasses and a shirt decorated in a pineapple motif. Outside, through a window, he could see the swimming pool, someone lying face down on a canvas chair.

"Yes," Edward replied. "I believe she didn't want to go back to England any more."

By two o'clock, Edward was told that he was free to leave. He had assured the police that he wanted to return home as soon as possible in order to break the news to his family and make preparations for Amy's funeral before the body arrived. In his room, he packed his own clothes but no others. He found he couldn't even bring himself to enter Amy's room, and resolved to tell the hotel to send the articles by mail. He also looked for Alice to say good-bye, but there was no answer from her room, and, as he was about to ask at the desk, he realized he didn't know her second name.

"If you give me her room number," the clerk said, "I might be able to help."

"Next to the Gable. You ought to remember her because she told me she'd been visiting here for years."

"There's someone called Liddell who usually stays next to the Gable."

"Red hair?"

"Yes."

A smile.

"But I haven't seen her for about ten days. I thought she had checked out."

"No. It must be someone else."

"Checked out temporarily. She often goes to another island."

"Her first name is Alice. She swims a lot."

"To visit a lover."

The clerk said this last remark in a whisper then smiled up at Edward adding, "What did you say her name was?"

"I didn't. It doesn't matter."

"A crazy woman in the Valentino was killed last night. Running away. Did you hear?"

Edward stared at him, then nodded. "Yes."

In his diary, as he awaited the time of his departure from the hotel, Edward tried to write down the events of the holiday as a form of therapy but gave up. *I suppose if I was a novelist,* he wrote finally, *I could make the story more dramatic, cutting out the day-to-day routine and concentrating on the action, the sensational, those things the public wants. But life isn't like that. Events, whether large or small, just happen, that's all.*

At five o'clock he was ready to leave, a suitcase in his hand, when there was a knock on the door. Edward hesitated, felt his face reddening, and almost ran to the door to open it. In the corridor stood Parkins and his wife.

"We thought we'd come with you to the airport," Parkins said. "It's the least we can do."

He then grinned and held on to the door frame.

Oh God, Edward thought, *they're drunk.*

In the taxi, Parkins and his wife sprawled in the back seat while Edward sat in front, next to the driver. He said hardly a word except a noncommittal yes or no according to the gibberish of conversation. He heard Henrietta talking about Burnstow, and that she would write down their address, and that it was by the sea. She was sure Edward would like it, and they would prepare the guest-room *comme ça.* Edward stared blankly through the windscreen, grateful only for the fact that this vulgar distraction delayed his solitude.

As they approached the airport, on one of the few serviceable roads, he heard Parkins talk about the crash. His wife tried to caution him but Parkins ignored her. He was now drinking from a hip-flask.

"I read that it was something to do with the fact that only here and somewhere off Japan does the compass needle point to *true* north rather than magnetic north. That's why all these accidents keep happening. Boats disappearing. Planes crashing."

"Aren't the butterflies too pretty?" Henrietta said, smiling, lowering the window.

"There was another bloody crash at the last place. Remember that, Edward?"

"Yes."

"It was in all the island papers."

"Was it?" Edward asked. He could now see the customs shed and the main runway.

"Must have been after you left. Front page. Well, what else have they got to write about?"

Edward looked at Parkins and said, "Had they found the bodies?"

"Oh, please," Henrietta said. "Let's not be so morbid. Edward doesn't want to talk about—"

"Had they?" Edward repeated.

"Not when we left. The buggers were quarrelling about how much they were to be paid."

"But they knew who he was? The man?"

"What? Oh yes. Of course they did. Some Spaniard."

"Spaniard?"

"Spaniard or Italian. His name sounded Spanish."

"Or Brazilian," Henrietta said.

"Well, what's the difference? Foreign anyway."

"You don't remember what it was?" Edward asked.

"No. Should I?"

"Nobody famous," Henrietta said. "Nobody worth mentioning."

Edward turned back and faced towards the front.

"Of course," Parkins added. "There were *two* people who died on the plane at Revenants. But then you knew that."

The taxi was now following the arrows to the Departure Lounge, moving between palm trees.

"There was a girl as well," Parkins said.

"English," added Henrietta.

"Yes. English, poor thing."

"*Pauvre jeune fille.*"

The Boeing was scheduled to fly to Miami, where Edward would transfer to another plane to London. It was three-quarters full and Edward sat near the back among two rows of empty seats, staring at the tarmac. The flight had been delayed, the Parkinses had lingered. Henrietta had spilt yet another drink ("God, I'm sorry. Absolutely *de trop*"), and then Edward finally was alone. It was a merciful peace. He thought once again of England, and if this is now a cliché, there are no apologies. Of all the countries in the world (and he had seen many), there was nowhere to which he would rather return. Especially at a time like this. He felt saddened by it, certainly, hating the fact that others—Americans, Europeans—considered it no more than a pathetic anachronism, sinking slowly into its silver sea. But then they were not English and never would be, no matter how hard they tried.

"Edward."

189 The Ninth Day

He thought of Amy as well. And of their absurd marriage, room next to room. And yet that also never offended anyone, except perhaps each other. At times, they really *were* the best of friends.

"Edward."

He thought also, of course, about Azevedo.

"Edward."

Full of dainty hungers.

"Edward."

He didn't move. He had heard the voice, his name being called, but he didn't move. He recognized who was calling him—it seemed to be just behind him as if a latecomer had just entered the aircraft—but he didn't turn around. He was conscious of the scream of jets, of the Boeing beginning to move forward, saw someone standing very still in a cornfield, waving. And then he smelt the perfume, the familiar odour of musk and decay that had been present in the dress in the bathroom, and he knew now where he had noticed it before. It had lingered in the T-shirt, even in the bikini. It was such a silly thing to happen. *I have to be back at work on Monday.*

He sensed her sit down next to him, leaning towards him. *There were TWO people who died in the plane at Revenants. But then you knew that.*

"Hello" said Alice.

For the Curious

Page ix: The quotation is by Charles Dana Gibson.

Page 5: The quotation is from *Panama* by Blaise Cendrars, translated from the French by John Dos Passos.

Page 26: Edward is alluding to the story, "The Devoted Widow" by Ambrose Bierce.

Page 43: The speech is from the film *Four Daughters*. Screenplay by Julius J. Epstein and Lenore Coffee (Warner Bros. 1938).

Page 89: The quotation is from *Quelque Chose Au Coeur* by Ford Madox Ford, translated from the English by Jacques Papy.

Page 94: The quotation is from *La Fin d'une Liaison* by Graham Greene, translated from the English by Marcelle Sibon.

Page 133: The extract is from the film *Singin' in the Rain*. Screenplay by Comden and Green (MGM).

Page 152: The Spanish quotation is from *Under the Volcano* by Malcolm Lowry.

Page 170: Parkins is referring to the story "The Blue Aspic" by Edward Gorey.

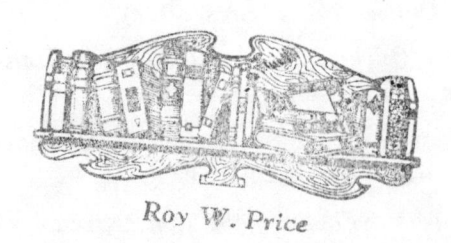

Roy W. Price